THE EMER/
AND OTHER DE

FÉLICIEN CHAMPSAUR (1858-1934) was a prolific French novelist and journalist. A core member of Émile Goudeau's literary club, the Hydropathes, he later became, through his own periodical, *Le Panurge*, loosely aligned with key figures of the Decadent Movement, such as Jean Lorrain and Rachilde. Though writing novels in a number of different veins, and attempting to establish himself as a "serious novelist" he was never able to shake off his reputation as a composer of risqué romances and erotic fantasies, a reputation that was not at odds with his public image. His novel *The Latin Orgy* was previously published by Snuggly Books, in a translation by Brian Stableford.

BRIAN STABLEFORD has been publishing fiction and non-fiction for fifty years. His fiction includes an eighteen-volume series of "tales of the biotech revolution" and a series of half a dozen metaphysical fantasies set in Paris in the 1840s, featuring Edgar Poe's Auguste Dupin. His most recent non-fiction projects are *New Atlantis: A Narrative History of British Scientific Romance* (Wildside Press 2016) and *The Plurality of Imaginary Worlds: The Evolution of French roman scientifique* (Black Coat Press 2016); in association with the latter he has translated approximately a hundred and fifty volumes of texts not previously available in English, similarly issued by Black Coat Press.

SNUGGLY BOOKS

FÉLICIEN CHAMPSAUR

THE EMERALD PRINCESS
AND OTHER DECADENT FANTASIES

Translated and with an Introduction by
Brian Stableford

THIS IS A SNUGGLY BOOK

ISBN: 978-1-943813-51-3

Contents

Introduction

L A PRINCESSE ÉMERAUDE by Félicien Champsaur (1858–1934), here translated as "The Emerald Princess," was first published in 1928 by Ferenczi et fils. It was a product of the final phase of the author's long career, which had begun in the late 1870s while he was still a student; he maintained a steady production thereafter until 1930, not long before his death, with only a brief interruption during the early years of the Great War.

The novella that forms the bulk of the present collection is one of the more whimsical productions of a rather self-indulgent period of Champsaur's career, and is by no means the only work of that period to contain a strong element of nostalgia, deliberately harking back to the stylistic extravagances of the Decadent Movement. It is a belated addition to the rich tradition of *femme fatale* stories associated with that Movement, which carried forward a tradition begun by Théophile Gautier, in his classic novellas *La Morte amoureuse* (1836; tr. as *Clarimonde*) and *Une Nuit de Cléopâtre* (1838; tr. as *One of Cleopatra's Nights*) and was extended by many other hands before losing impetus somewhat after the addition of such early-twentieth-century exemplars as Camille Mauclair's *Le Poison de pierries* (1903; tr. as *The Poison of Precious Stones*).

La Princesse émeraude is one of numerous stories in that tradition to draw on the mythological figure of the lamia, which became entangled in French legendry with the story of the snake-woman Mélusine, based on a thirteenth-century romance only known in retrospective summary, if it ever really existed. Typically for Champsaur, when deliberately tackling familiar themes with familiar narrative strategies, he wanted to produce a version of the story that was unusually flamboyant and extreme, and although the novella is a trifle slapdash—he always made up his plots as he went along, sometimes leading to defects of organization and, as in the present case, odd instances of forgetfulness—it is certainly not lacking in melodramatic brio and striking imagery. Its lurid symbolism is certainly less polished than that deployed in many of its more august predecessors, but the story retains the quasi-primitive charm that distinguishes so many of the author's engagingly bizarre fantasies.

The stories juxtaposed with the novella in the present volume all date from a much earlier phase in Champsaur's career. "Le Petit-Fils de Faust" (tr. as "Faust's Grandson"), "Ballade du Tramway" (tr. as "The Fantastic Tram," Champsaur having retitled the story "Le Tramway fantastique" in the second edition) and "Le Perroquet incrédule" (tr. as "The Incredulous Parrot") were all first collected in book form in the edition of *Entrée de Clowns* published by Jules Lévy in an edition dated 1885. The collection appeared shortly after the author's second novel, *Miss America* (1885), and did not actually become available until the early months of 1886, perhaps delayed by the late arrival of some of its lavish illustrations.

"La Mystérieuse" (tr. as "The Mystery Woman") was newly added to the second edition of that collection, issued by La Nouvelle Revue Critique in 1926, but the story originally dates from the 1880s, when Champsaur was still writing the occasional item adapted to fit snugly into a newspaper *feuilleton* slot. He soon gave up such work, because he was too fluent and verbose a writer to be able to adapt readily to the routine production of stories of the requisite length of 1,500-1,800 words, but the examples included here demonstrate that he had all the narrative devices at his disposal that had been developed in association with that peculiar artistry. All four short stories were written while Champsaur was still associated with Émile Goudeau's Hydropathes, hanging out at Le Chat Noir, and enjoying the lifestyle enthusiastically depicted in his first novel, *Dinah Samuel* (1882); they reflect various aspects of the spirit of that time and place, developed in a flirtatiously mischievous fashion.

Pierrot et sa conscience (tr. as "Pierrot and his Conscience"), was initially published, like *La Princesse émeraude*, in a small illustrated volume, in this instance a very lavish if somewhat insubstantial volume published by Dentu in 1896. Like the shorter stories that precede it, it is very much a product of the *fin-de-siècle*, but more self-consciously so; indeed, it is one of the products of the period most heavily saturated with an elegiac sense of a deflated and exhausted era coming to an end. The mischievous merriment of the earlier stories has largely evaporated in the novelette, and what remains is a sorrowful and regretful disenchantment, which contrasts sharply with the buoyant mood of the earlier works while refusing to let go of their attitude and wit.

Champsaur subsequently issued a much expanded version of *Pierrot et sa conscience* as the novella *Nuit de fête* (Offenstadt frères, 1902), but precisely because the expanded version was published after the beginning of the new century, it looks back at the end of the previous era from a markedly differently viewpoint, which adds an extra dimension to its cynicism but loses something of the poignancy of the original version. The longer version added a good deal of satirical material referring more elaborately and more specifically to Champsaur's contemporaries, somewhat after the fashion of *Dinah Samuel*, but the shorter original has a charm, a light touch and an economy atypical of Champsaur's work, which help to make it remarkable.

Like many of the authors who seemed at the time to be exemplary of the *fin-de-siècle* sensibility, Champsaur had, to some extent, to reinvent himself when the new century began, and he did so more successfully than most, aided by the impetus given to him by the bestselling status that he had first achieved with *L'Amant des danseuses* [*The Man Who Loved Dancing-Girls*] (1888). In the final year of the century he produced *Lulu: roman clownesque* (1900), a novelization of a pantomime contemporary with *L'Amant des danseuses* and dealing with the same theme, which became his summary farewell to that phase of his career. Although he changed tack and tactics thereafter, deliberately indulging in a geographical and historical exoticism that took him far away from his Parisian stamping ground, to the Far East, in *Poupée japonaise* [*Japanese Doll*] (1900) and the "Hindu novel" *Le Semeur d'amour* [*The Sower of Amour*] (1902), and then to ancient Rome in *L'Orgie Latine* (1903; tr. as *The Latin Orgy*), he never lost contact with his quintessentially

Parisian Decadent sensibility, and he certainly never lost his fascination with *femmes fatales*.

In consequence of that long fidelity, *La Princesse émeraude* can be regarded as a kind of culmination of a long series of such stories spanning his entire career, and, indeed, the illustration used as a frontispiece in the book, by an artist long associated with his works, Lucien Jaquelux, depicts the author surrounded by a collection of his creations, all of them exotically and archetypally beautiful women, except for the unhuman hero of *Ouha, roi des singes* (1922; tr. as *Ouha, King of the Apes*). The artist supplied a supplementary pictorial key on the facing page, obligingly identifying the literary sources of the six women depicted in the frontispiece itself and adding three more images to complete a set of imaginary Muses, including Dinah Samuel, Lulu, the Empress Messaline from *L'Orgie Latine* and half a dozen others.

La Princesse émeraude is not, however, merely one more bead in a chaplet, but represents a deliberate attempt by the author to go beyond anything he had done before, in producing a kind of ultimate *femme fatale*, a symbolic summation of the species. Djila, the Emerald Princess, was not the last of his images of ultimately desirable women, being followed a year later by the eponymous heroine of *Nora, la guenon devenue femme* (1929; tr. as *Nora, the Ape-Woman*). A dancing-girl of a baser nature than the idealized Lulu, Nora represents a bitter nostalgia of a different kind, and although she is archetypal in her fashion, she does not have the kind of ultimate glamour that the author attempted to embody in Djila. *La Princesse émeraude* is a considerably less elaborate work than *L'Orgie Latine* and a considerably less affectionate one than *Lulu*, partly because of its deliberate mock-Gallandesque stylization, but that same stylization also gives it a mock-epic quality that none of Champsaur's early works in that vein were able to attain, and a curious kind of grandiosity.

✳

The translation of *La Princesse émeraude* was made from a copy of the Ferenczi edition. The translations of the first four short stories were made from the copy of the 1926 edition of *Entrée de Clowns* reproduced on the Bibliothèque Nationale's *gallica* website, although comparative reference was also made to the 1885 edition reproduced on the same website, in order to note a few additions to the later versions. The translation of *Pierrot et sa conscience* was made from the copy of the Dentu edition reproduced on the Internet Archive website at archive.org.

Brian Stableford

THE EMERALD PRINCESS
AND OTHER DECADENT FANTASIES

Faust's Grandson

HE had just attended a performance of Gounod's masterpiece, *Faust*. After a trip to the club, where he had ended up losing the last of his money, the grandson of the celebrated doctor went home very sad, for he was in love with Alice Penthièvre, and, after the performance, he had seen her climb into a cab with her old ape. Yes, she had left him for a player on the Bourse who, having profited to the tune of a million and a half in his speculations on the famous Societé Bontoux, had had a good enough nose to sniff the impending collapse and liquidate.

On emerging from the gambling den, Faust's grandson had admired the moon, like a *louis d'or* cast into the night, a discreet procuress drawing the starry curtain over the amorous, and now he was writing a sonnet whose rhymes had buzzed in his cranium as he walked through the streets:

The Battles of Life[1]

Twenty, at the most, sleeping beside an old man
Greedy for her soft skin and brazen attitude;

---

1 Because the story specifically refers to the sonnet's rhymes I have contrived a version that retains the rhyme scheme rather than translating each line literally, hopefully reproducing the spirit and doggerel quality of the original.

Her long blonde hair, and her body, in the nude
Extends languidly for him on the soft divan.

The darling's bag is stuffed by a financier
Almost impotent, who found her flat broke;
But the métier's hard, enough to choke
The blonde, fed up with something chancier.

She has to earn that house on the avenue
The little whore, adorable and true,
Trying in vain her old lover to excite.

Will she be disgusted by the old gray beard
And the groping of virility disappeared
When she wakes in the morning after tonight?

When he had finished the last line, with his elbows on the table and his head in his hands, he thought at first of the folly of millions agitating Paris, and then about his ancestor.

People are no longer as naive as that doctor. He claimed to know everything: philosophy, law, medicine and theology too, but if he had had another distraction in his work than invoking Phoebe, summoning her mild and melancholy amity, if he had studied life, instead of poring, almost incessantly, over dusty books, he would not have demanded that Mephistopheles, in exchange for his soul, give him youth. When the Devil offered him a fortune, the doctor had not had insults enough for gold and its pleasures.

Youth has all the privileges? Those who imagine that can look to see whether they have gold coins in their pockets and banknotes in their wallet . . . Supernatural apparitions are no longer abreast of the times, for if the Devil consented to show himself now, Faust's grandson would gladly sell him any soul he might have in order to obtain opulence and old age.

As he was reflecting in this fashion, he heard a light sound of footsteps and, directing his gaze toward the entrance door, he perceived a very distinguished stranger, who, after bowing, approached him and handed him a card, on which were engraved, beneath a closed crown, the words:

Prince de Satan

The young man invited the visitor to sit down and presented him with a box of cigars, inviting his to take one.

"Forgive me, Monsieur," he added, "but what proof do I have that you really are the Devil?"

Satan took a few state-manufactured matches from the mantelpiece and, strike after strike, lit seven of them in succession.

It was extraordinary.

Faust's grandson, convinced by that evident manifestation of a superior and mysterious power, spoke in the following terms:

"My grandfather, who had the honor of making a deal with you, delivered his soul to you in exchange for your having rendered him young, in answer to his desire. He was able to be content to flirt with Marguerite and see—which he would not have been able to do when he was buried in his books—more charms in her half-closed eyelids and her fresh lips than in all the wisdom in the world. I, Faust's grandson, am young, and yet I don't esteem that it's much preferable to having lived.

"A man, during his childhood, is ignorant of everything. Afterwards, he uses up his youth, and also his maturity, in efforts that are sometimes not crowned with success, in order to acquire comfort and fortune for his old age. An employee obtains his retirement—which is to say, happiness—after thirty years of submission and regularity. A merchant becomes a rentier after wasting the best part of his existence in a shop. A soldier receives, when it is too late, the epaulettes of a general admired by beautiful ladies and saluted by gentlemen. An artist, painter, musician, writer or sculptor, does not have renown or success, and, above all, does not possess the fortune for which he dreamed in order to satisfy his aristocratic caprices—for any artist worthy of the name is an aristocrat—until his hair turns white, when his youth has fled, many winters ago, weeping in the midst of illusions.

"That is why, Monsieur, little desirous of remaining in difficulty, impatient to arrive at enjoyment and the goal, I would be delighted, if you could grant it to me—of which I have no doubt—to be respectably old and a millionaire, immediately."

Mephistopheles, who was smoking his cigar, had listened to Faust's grandson in the most polite fashion, for he had lent him scrupulous attention; but he had certainly known in advance everything that the young man had to confide in him. In a familiar tone, he said:

"I divine, my dear fellow, that you are under the hammer of the eternal question of amour and money. You have spent quite a bit of money, thirty thousand francs—all that you had—in a month, on Alice Penthièvre of the Avenue de Messine, and, as you are now cleaned out, you have been surpassed.

"You are not one of those lovers who go in via the kitchen and up by the service stairway. I congratulate you all the more for that, as I am glad to inform you that it has been decided this evening in the Council of Ministers— which I attended in the skin of Monsieur Grévy[1]—that the Prefect of Police will be given the mission of purging Paris of at least ten thousand pimps. The project has been drawn up of forming three exceptional regiments, which will be sent overseas in order to terminate the Tonkin affair. They will, moreover, retain their distinctive character and will have a superb, tightly fitting green costume, brandeburgs and tall helmets. Grévin[2] will design the uniforms for the three regiments. That way, we shall put an end to those ridiculous Chinamen. If Monsieur Grévy accepts the Council's decision, the foreign news section of the newspapers will soon be full of reports of triumphs: *Great naval combat. The three-tier helmets continue to cover themselves with glory* . . .

"In Paris, as you see, my dear, the Devil must be everywhere. It's exhausting, take my word for it. But let's get back to our affair. You want to be immensely rich. Doubtless in order that the slightest caprices of one or several women can be executed; you want to be opulent and old right away. I consent to that. What will you cede to me in return?"

"My soul. It will be deliverable to you by contract, whenever it pleases God to separate it from my body."

Satan forgot all discretion and uttered a burst of laughter on a shrill note.

---

1 Jules Grévy was the President of the Republic from 1879-1887.
2 The caricaturist Alfred Grévin (1827-1892) was also a prolific designer of theatrical costumes.

"Your soul, did you say? That's too droll. Let's try to talk a little more seriously, shall we?"

He went on:

"The soul exists. It is tradeable, but the stock is not high. Once, a hundred years ago, I speculated a great deal on that commodity. Souls went from five hundred francs to seven hundred, then twelve hundred, and finally to three thousand. However, I went through severe crises without flinching when Locke, Condillac and Kant, who searched for the soul in the fluid contained in the cerebral cavities, declared that every idea is a continued sensation, and when Voltaire said, smiling, that *soul* is a word invented to express, confusedly and obscurely, the mechanisms of our life.

"I resisted all those attacks, but then came, after those of Cabanis, the experiments of Magendie and Flourens, those of Sir John Lubbock, Bain and Huxley in England, of Berthelot, Broca, Robin, Vulpian and d'Orbigny in France. Friedreich wrote that the same force that digests via the stomach thinks via the brain, Littré that mind is a property of the nervous substance, as gravitation is of every material particle . . .

"A collapse was threatened. I should have suspected as much; souls crashed. I took a heavy hit. But I have the stomach and I absorbed the blow. Even so, a scalded Devil fears cold water. I don't want your soul! Why do these so-called scientists have so much influence? From first to last, though, they're only spinning out, in bad prose, this distich from the grotesque poet Cyrano de Bergerac:

An hour after death, our soul is in dearth,
Become what it was an hour before birth.

"You'll understand, therefore, that I can't accept your soul, since its distinction from the body is, for humans, a simple analytical procedure. But I can take your youth. You have twenty years, black and supple hair, soft and energetic eyes. If you wish, I'll acquire all of that, in order to lead astray some chaste girl—not on earth, of course, for no young woman here any longer believes in silliness, and virgins here no longer allow themselves to be cajoled by sweet talk, but on other worlds that are more backward than your planet and where chimeras have not yet become ridiculous . . .

"In return for the abandonment you make me, you'll obtain what you would scarcely have had, by dint of labor, in thirty years: old age and fortune. The means is facile. I've always known what scientists would eventually discover after centuries. Claude Bernard explains, in his studies on the problem of physiology, that by injecting oxygenated blood via the carotid into the head of a decapitated dog, one sees the vital properties of the muscles, glands, nerves and the brain slowly return. If you permit me to operate, my dear, *in anima nobile*, I can oxygenate you to the point of saturation and you'll live forty years in the space of five minutes . . .

"Will you sell me your youth? I hope to utilize that cast-off clothing on one of the other planets rotating around your sum."

After a silence, the young man said:

"I'll gladly accept to be old and to possess for myself alone the beloved who is escaping me . . . Penthièvre— which astonishes me, for she has intelligence—is capable, then, of sticking to me . . . By the way, you know, I don't want an inconvenient passion. It's sufficient that I find

9

a tranquil and delightful amour in the evening, at ten or eleven o'clock, after the club."

"As you please."

"Shall we sign the pact, then?"

So Faust's grandson sold his youth, was sixty years old and, what is more, stole Alice Penthièvre from the stock-market trader enriched by Monsieur Bontoux's disaster. His blonde lover deceived him with a young assistant stockbroker, but as he never knew anything about it, he was very happy.

And he even remained young, because, as soon as she saw them appear, she plucked out his white hairs.

The Mystery Woman

A ND because that woman had gone, his soul, once again, was plunged into a moral limbo from which he could not extract it.

Did he sincerely want to do so, in fact?

The anxious question that he asked himself remained without a precise response. He wanted that, oh, yes, he wanted it . . . but something gripped him, an appetite for voluptuous suffering. Was he incorrigible, then? From time to time, he delighted in dolor; it was his intellectual malady—a malady that he nursed.

She, precisely by her amiability, by her delicate, aristocratic and infantile mischievousness, had cured him of it or, at least, had preserved him for a long time from a relapse. It was not spleen, leaden ennui, from which he suffered thus; on the contrary, he did not go a minute without the collision of ideas in his overtaxed mind. He had worked too hard. He was not exhausted, for, on the contrary, he had developed some of his mental faculties in an abnormal manner. Curious about thought, the secrets of nature and life, the brains, passions, lusts and ambitions in conflict around him, his nerves sang excessively at the slightest friction, like those Aeolian harps that are placed high up on houses and whose mourning or laughing strings make cheerful or sad chords heard in the slightest breeze.

He finally took account of the fact that he desired, above all, the infinite happiness of suffering, sharper vibrations never attained and always desired, in spite of his immense fear, which had itself served as a joy: an embrace clenching his brain, indescribable hours in which he was invaded by the unknown.

She had said to him: "Until Thursday!" Not the next one, oh no, but in a fortnight's time! She had never left it so long without visiting him. The pretext: a necessary absence, a voyage.

Now, he knew nothing about her except the little, true or false, that she had told him. He could not find her in Paris or seek her out discreetly. He did not know her address, which she had not given him. He always wrote to her *poste restante*. Who was she, in society and in life? To what class did she belong? Was she married, divorced, or kept? He had thought, by virtue of her elegance, sometimes a trifle eccentric, that she was maintained. About intercourse she knew everything, but that was not a reason. Then again, he knew them all, the prominent courtesans, or at least those in view. He would surely have encountered her in places of pleasure. Whereas, he knew nothing about her—the intermittent mystery woman—but her infinite loveliness, all of her patrician body, the smallest creases of the satin of her skin, and a forename, a dainty diminutive: Gaby.

And perhaps also her thinking, since, little by little, in the year that they had loved one another, he had detached her from her childish haze, and Gaby was very different, on certain days, from the pretty bird that he had captured one evening for the first time. That one had only known how to smooth her feathers and to sing, and her linnetesque twittering had only served to make her admired.

She had intelligence, in the Parisian sense of the word: the intelligence that the lightest minds assimilate, contained in an apposite smile showing fine white teeth. He had discovered her soul and had shown her "it."

A fortnight to wait! An inexpressible anguish squeezed his breast. However, she had quit him with an amiable kiss: a sincere kiss, he thought. Was it really honest, without a hidden agenda, that slightly distracted kiss? She had been in haste to depart, anxious about the possibility of being late. She thought about things of which he knew nothing while giving herself to him. Perhaps she was thinking abut another man, another more important than him to her, at the moment?

No, that was impossible, absurd. He was becoming jealous. Oh, jealous of her, about whom he knew nothing, of whom he only had a few hours from time to time. He was torturing himself *"à plaisir."* That banal expression, *"à plaisir,"* how true it was; torturing himself *"à plaisir."*[1]

Yes, it was still an enjoyment, that torture; he had created it. They had already separated, however, many times, but this was not the same. When she had quit him, the other times, he had still sensed her close to him; she had left him, at home in his bachelor apartment, something subtle that was "Her."

What obliged her to such a long absence?

It was necessary, for her to have said adieu to him like that this time, that she loved someone else—the redoubtable "Other" whose menacing shadow he had always sensed floating over them.

---

1 The *double entendre* in this phrase does not translate; it can mean "without restriction" or recklessly as well as, more obviously, "with pleasure" or delightedly.

And suddenly, the idea of "the Other" was magnified within him—of the man who, perhaps, had taken her definitively—and also that of an irremediable solitude: a frightful, eternal solitude, it seemed, now that she had gone.

Alone, he was all alone.

To go out, to see friends, to run around the swarming, noisy city, where gaieties and indifferences aggravated his sadness further, to mingle with Paris agitated by joys, chagrins and fevers? Today, he was incapable of it. And then, that would be even sadder, the solitude in the crowd, the throng that he now hated.

The Other?

He took his head in his hands, in order to reflect, to know—if he could at least succeed in imagining—the enemy. Was the Other perhaps a husband? Or a lover she had had for a long time, the man who enabled her to live? But she declared herself to be independent, even letting it be understood that she possessed a certain fortune.

And what if she did not come back, that Thursday? Not knowing where to find her, what would he do? How could he struggle against the Other, ungraspable, of whom he knew nothing, neither the rank, nor the beauty or ugliness, nor the intelligence, nor the wealth or poverty? He did not know what place he might occupy in her heart, in her head, in her linnetesque existence.

Atrociously jealous because she had gone, he feared having lost his dream forever. It was simply that she had filled a great void within him, that woman—not that she was less banal than many other women who had disappointed him, but she was very beautiful and very good; at first he had cherished her for that, without giving the sentiment any great cerebral range.

Then it had been necessary to bring forth from that exquisitely pretty and modern woman a personality contrasting with his own melancholy; he had been attached profoundly by that contrast, which brought him back from his pessimisms. He had loved her seductive and mischievous chatter, her diversity and her caprices, often original.

In sum, she completed him, he being rather serious and grave, with her gaiety of a little bird in spring, amused by a butterfly.

This time, he sensed that she had taken away "Her" soul, and his own soul too, for they were narrowly linked. And if she came back later, he imagined that it would doubtless be Her, but an entirely different woman, because her soul would have remained out there, where she had gone.

Finally, that Thursday so desired and so feared had arrived. It was the appointed day, the hour, the same hour when she had entered his home the first time, with a gloved hand on the fine black veil and on the little red mouth: "Shh! It's me! Never tell anyone!" Now, he listened to his heart beating, as, during nights of insomnia, the ticking of a clock beats time to the diffuse thoughts of a semi-dream.

The bell rang loudly. He ran to open the door himself. Her! It was Her! Gaby!

Alert, slender, very cheerful, ravishing, after allowing herself to be kissed on the eyelids, on the lips and among the meager curls of her nape, where her feminine odor intoxicated him, she threw her hat on to the divan, and unfastened her coat with pretty childlike gestures. Chattering, she adjusted the mauve petals of a cattleya pinned to her corsage. Already she was recounting some little adventure, joking about people he did not know, whom she imitated, babbling about this and that.

She was happy, insouciant, she had "heaps of things" to tell him. And he looked at her, bewildered. It was true; she was no longer the casual mistress of the other day. She was a stranger who only resembled Her . . .

And suddenly, he cried: "But it's no longer you!"

She burst out laughing, blonde, with a fringe of soft curls around her forehead, amethyst eyes, streaked with gold, under long lashes, the tempting mouth, a partly open flower.

"No longer me? You're crazy!"

"No, it's no longer you. You've left your soul out there, and mine too, which you took from me, the last time, when you went away. He's stolen them—*the Other!*"

She defied him, strong in her loveliness, the attraction of her blonde hair, her red lips, and her air of saying: *I'm only my own, but you, who look at me with that desire, belong to me, in spite of everything.*

With a further burst of laughter, she stung him, gracefully:

"*The Other?* And why not *the others*, my dear?"

The Fantastic Tram

(A great German poet will translate this ballad. I
have not yet been able to calculate in what year;
the number is immeasurable.)

THE driver was asleep because he had drunk a great
deal, the previous evening, with his friends, in honor
of the national festival of the fourteenth of July, 1880—
but that was not too inconvenient, the horses being used
to marching between the rails.

He was a terrible driver, Pantinois, the driver of the
tram from La Villette to L'Étoile. A friend of artists and
loose women, when he had been a simple cab driver he
had carried Dinah Samuel twice and Victor Hugo once.
He had a long beard, an enormous mouth, a grandiose
nose, immense eyes and vast ears, with golden curls.

He was a handsome coachman, a complete beau, a
bachelor of letters.

Behind him came the tram, which seemed the continu-
ation of, a kind of bizarre development of, the man. The
driver was gray,[1] the tram was yellow, and the two of them,

---

1 The French *gris* [gray] also means "drunk," while *jaune* [yellow] is
the color of envy in that language. I have translated the former word
literally here in order to preserve the wordplay, but have translated its
metaphorical meaning subsequently.

who appeared to make a single whole, were going along the Boulevard de Courcelles, dreaming.

It was five o'clock in the evening.

At one time, the driver, raising his eyelids toward his bushy brown eyebrows, perceived an oxygenated courtesan passing close to them, in a victoria, her torso tipped back nonchalantly on a cushion. On each door was painted, in gold, the initial of the beauty's name: Q.

Beneath it, also in gold, shone the motto: *Hence my fortune.*

The drunken coachman peered at the blonde courtesan, went to sleep, saw her again in a dream; and the yellow tram followed her. Perhaps it would be necessary to have short trousers and pointed shoes to have that chick. The coachman would have her anyway! But, truly, he had just enough lucidity to pull up at the stops and set off again at the conductor's signal.

Such is his adventure:

Gradually, the little lady felt ill at ease. Why was the coachman looking at her like that? Suddenly, as if wanting to escape a fascination, she had her horses whipped, which started to gallop.

They are in the Avenue de Wagram. The drunken driver, quite simply, whips his horses too. The tram matches the pace of the victoria.

The little lady was pretty, and the driver was drunk.

The Rue de l'Étoile opens to the right. The victoria turns into it. The tram cannot quit the track; the dainty blonde is saved. No! Pantinois braces himself, tugs the reins, cracks his whip, and also turns into the Rue de l'Étoile.

The victoria takes the Rue de Ternes and the Rue de Villiers; the tram also takes the Rue de Ternes and the Rue de Villiers, and goes through the gate.

The victoria flees, frightened. The tram runs behind, with a metallic noise sounding on the roadway. The victoria, more and more frightened, turns left at a street corner, toward Puteaux.

The passengers do not know what to think.

A hectic race commences. The victoria goes through the villages of the suburbs at top speed, and the tram still follows, progressing in jolts and bounds. Pantinois, impassively, keeps his eyes on the little blonde.

Well, you know what coachmen are like.

The little blonde, pale and all atremble, cuts through space in her victoria. One is not afraid of a man, however, especially a foreigner. Now, the drunken driver is Belgian. The passengers are bewildered.

Fougères, fields of wheat, flax, barley, rape, oats, maize, mustard, hemp, millet, potatoes, beets, buckwheat, rye and saffron; cemeteries planted with chestnut trees and willows; squares of celeriac, lettuces, turnips, parsley, cabbages and carrots; streams bordered with slender poplars; villages, towns, hills, plains, parks, ponds, hawthorn hedges and rose bushes; meadows, peasants of both sexes and russet cows lying in the grass, all file past them with a prodigious rapidity.

Sometimes, immense forests bar the route, but the victoria and the tram go on regardless. Just as a bullet, fired at close range at a pane of glass, sometimes only makes a round hole, so the victoria and the tram traverse the woods, cutting straight through the trunks, breaking off branches, stripping leaves and making a tunnel. They leave a strange parallelepiped in the forest.

Their passage is a vision of a second. They go on, and on, and on. At times, conurbations, prefectures, sub-prefectures and the chief places of cantons appear. Frightened, they stop dead and present their steeples like the halberds of gatekeepers.

But they are slow, and remain on the defensive. The victoria and the tram do not penetrate their walls; the conurbations, prefectures, sub-prefectures and the chief places of cantons straighten their steeples, pricking the azure. Thus the Île-de-France and Touraine file past.

Hup! Hup! Make way, good people, make way!

At the same time as the Victoria and the tram, the daylight went away. Now the sun was setting, in the distance, toward the sea, in a great red shroud. Gradually, night descended, extending over the ground the shadows of telegraph poles.

The sun was dying, and things were blurred, one by one, by a vague dusk. The driver, without interrupting his vertiginous course, lit the headlights of the tram, glazed in red.

And the tram was now gazing at the victoria.

Hup! Hup! Faster! Hup! Hup! The tram is going to catch up with the victoria.

Not yet. They have arrived in Brittany, in a bleak plain. In the distance, on the horizon, a dull and lugubrious sound rises into the sky, against which crude and gigantic forms are outlined.

The victoria has just disappeared behind one of those tall and severe forms. There are thousands of them on the plain. The moon, half-hidden by a cloud, casts a livid light over all those monsters. The victoria is lost in their midst.

The driver of the tram sounds his horn, and soon, as far as the eye can see, dolmens, menhirs, rocking stones, covered paths and cromlechs, form several lines and make way. Now the tram is right behind the victoria again! The moon illuminates them.

Two passengers have gone insane.

Hup! Hup! The dead go quickly. Hup! Hup! Hup! The Ocean, behind a cliff, looms up and bellows. Hup! Hup! It's the end, the end in the foamy sea. Hup! Hup! The victoria has not stopped. It hurtles forward, and after it, the tram makes a leap. They go on, and on, skimming the white crests of the waves. Velocity has nullified weight!

(It is that observation, made by a poet long ago, in the 1880s, from which aeroplanes were born.)[1]

And they go on in that fashion for nights and days, nights and days, for years and centuries. The driver of the tram is still calm and placid, staring incessantly, blinking his eyes. He is the angel of the tram. The little courtesan is still blonde and beautiful, but her dress is no longer fashionable.

Hup! Hup! Darwin has said that plants and animals are transformed in accordance with the environments in which they live; the wheels of the victoria and the tram are transformed into fins. It is a mere matter of time, as Darwin knows full well.

Now, the sky.

They have crossed the seas and the continents thousands of times. Finally, the victoria and the tram, vanquishers of centripetal force, escape at a tangent and depart into space through the unlimited ether.

The years flow by, innumerable, and the victoria and the tram keep going, incessantly. They encounter the

---

1 This interjection was added to the 1926 edition of the story, being understandably absent from the version published in 1885. There are a few other trivial alterations, including the addition of the date 1880.

moon. The drunken driver sounds his horn again, as he did between La Villlette and L'Étoile, and the moon accelerates its revolution in order to make way.

One passenger is struck by aphasia. A female passenger, who has married during the journey, gives birth, painlessly, to a little boy. He is baptized, and when he is three years old, the conductor marks the occasion by ringing the bell.

Ding!

Further away, asteroids surge forth, planets and other moons. All of them make way.

The tram, whose fins have become wings, is no more than a few leagues from the victoria. The minx, caught, while dressed to the nines,[1] feels the coachman's whip on the fine down of her nape.

She turns her head, and, for the first time, the tram is disturbed.

The driver does not see a heavenly body passing in front of them, accomplishing its rotation around the sun, and forgets to sound his horn. The tram is traveling, like the victoria, at a speed of fifteen hundred meters a second when it suddenly stops.

A frightful impact! The tram has crashed into the rings of Saturn!

Then, Pantinois, no longer being lulled by the movement of the vehicle, wakes up completely, and murmurs, while shaking himself:

"Here's the Place de l'Étoile. The little minx must be at the Porte Dauphiné by now. All the same, I drank too much yesterday, in honor of the festival . . . and I think I have a headache."

---

1 There is an untranslatable pun here, developing two argot meanings of the repeated word *épinglée* [literally, pinned].

The Incredulous Parrot

PÉPIN DES GRILLONS, a freshly appointed Prefec-
torial Councilor, was chatting in the Café des Cigales
with Patrice Montclar, his childhood friend, who came
every year to spend a fortnight in the area. At table on
the terrace, behind a sheet of white cloth bordered with
wisteria, in the shade of the tall plane trees of the Cours,
they were both evoking stories of old while waiting for the
procession to go past.

Suddenly, Pépins des Grillons said:

"Do you remember Misè Sabine's parrot?"

"Yes, that Pentecost. Nanette and little Lalie were very
pretty. I remember, old chap. We were fourteen. Oh, that
parrot! It violated our first amours, and I'd gladly have
wrung its neck."

The impressions of the first flush of youth are marked
in the memory for a long time; others that are nobler, cru-
eler, more joyful or more ardent might be added to them
over time, but the old ones remain vivid and charming.

Certainly, Monclar—the Parisian, as he was nicknamed
in Grivesdesvignes—had not forgotten. The slightest de-
tails of the tableau of yore returned to his mind. In any
case, today as then, sheets perfumed with rosemary were
spread in the wardrobes and little bouquets distributed at

intervals displayed along the houses of the sunlit town; to-day, as then, the streets were strewn with flowers, syringas, carnations, and, above all, an efflorescence of roses.

It was truly droll.

Misè Sabine, the old woman, tall and thin, the candle-seller whose shop was on the Cours—the *s* is pronounced—had set up, opposite the Café Passeron, an elegant temporary altar, a nest of verdure.

She was supervising the work of Nanette and Lalie, prowling busily round their altar and placing, here and there, spider plants, spurges and martagon lilies, when the tailor Paticlet, who had been standing next to the devotee, open-mouthed, for five minutes with his hands in his pockets, pronounced in a definite manner:

"It's pretty, very pretty, your altar! I compliment you on it, Misè Sabine."

Paticlet was a malicious fellow, a diabolical joker.

"Isn't it, neighbor? Admit that it's arranged with rather good taste."

"Yes, but it lacks something."

"What's that?"

"What? You don't see it? In the midst of the moss it would go very well . . ."

"What are you talking about?" cried the candle-merchant, beginning to get impatient.

"You can do as you like, but if I were you, I'd put up there, at the top, a parrot—the one I have, for example. It would, I'm sure, produce a delightful effect." It was obvious that his suggestion was welcome. "I'll go and get it, Misè Sabine—I'll go right away."

After five minutes, the tailor came back, carrying his bird proudly. He placed the cage himself on top of the altar; then, addressing the idlers who were stationed there: "What do you think, you folks?"

And each of them exclaimed in admiration. "That goes very well," they said to Paticlet. "It goes very well . . . what a good idea you've had!"

The parrot, slightly alarmed, clicked its beak angrily, suspended from the bars. Afterwards, understanding that its new elevation posed no danger to it, it descended on to the perch. There, standing on one foot, it used the other to grab a sugar lump, and nibbled it with pretty movements of the head.

People were ecstatic. "How pleased Monsieur le Curé will be!"

The curé was Monsieur Cougourdon,[1] the former director of a little seminary, a worthy man who could be seen during the week in his little house in Sièyes with his soutane tucked up, playing skittles. In devoting himself to that exercise with his notable neighbors, Monsieur Testanière, the justice of the peace, Monsieur Andrelait and Monsieur Pivert, he did not believe that he was decreasing his prestige. He was going to have enough of that today! He was standing in for the bishop in the procession, the latter being then in Paris, in the Minister's antechamber.

Paticlet, meanwhile, was rubbing his hands.

Misè Sabine had left with Lalie and Nanette to go to

---

1 Monsieur Courgordon, during his days as a schoolmaster, as well as the two friends reminiscing about their youth here, also features in another story in the first edition of *Entrée de Clowns*, "La Leçon de catéchisme," which was dropped from the 1926 version. Grivesdesvignes [literally vine-thrushes] is presumably a transfiguration of Turriers [which name could, by a stretch of the imagination, be likened to *Turdus*, the Latin name of the thrush genus] in the Basses-Alpes, where the author grew up.

the church. The bells were ringing full-tilt, announcing that the procession was setting forth.

"Here it comes! Here it comes!" cried Misè Margoton to a few saintly women who had remained beside the altar—and she immediately threw incense on to a brazier placed behind the geranium pots.

The little girls from the Sisters' school were marching at the head of the procession. The youngest were wearing baskets full of rose petals and golden genista flowers around their necks, held by blue ribbons. All of them, dainty in their white dresses, with their hair loose, were singing:

> *Gentle Mary,*
> *Sovereign of Heaven,*
> *Dear Mother,*
> *Patron of this place,*
> *Watch over our childhood,*
> *Protect our innocence,*
> *Save that precious wealth.*

Then came the pupils of the Brothers of the Christian Doctrine. They advanced, their arms swinging, stiff in their Sunday clothes, and they all stopped, open-mouthed, in front of the temporary altar.

"A parrot!" they whispered. "A parrot! How handsome it is!"

And they stood there, in ecstasy. But old Symmaque, the director, shouted in his loud voice: "Forward, boys!"

Here comes the congregation of the Immaculate Conception. Four young girls are carrying the statue of the Holy Virgin, under which women pass back and forth, holding children in their arms, to summon the protection of the Good Mother. The chorists, Nanette and Lalie among them, detach themselves from the cortège and come to take up a position beside the temporary altar for a canticle before the benediction.

Montclar and Pépin des Grillons, buttoned up in their school uniforms, their faces puffed up, are devouring the group of girls with their eyes. How those white dresses suit them! How gracious they are, the pleats of those transparent veils! And the arms whose troubling skin can be seen through the muslin!

The gray penitents might be singing *Laudate* at the tops of their voices, but Patrice and Pépin des Grillons can neither hear them nor see them; they cannot perceive anything but Nanette and Lalie, and the commencements of their new breasts beneath a light ruche.

Monsieur le Curé finally arrives in front of the altar and kneels down.

The parrot, immobile on its perch, very calm while the procession field past, appears very interested in the ceremony in the process of unfurling before it; it listens gravely, without opening it beak, to the pious canticle intoned by the demoiselles, a little *allegro* quite catchy and slightly naughty:

I sense his presence!
Heaven is within me!
My soul in silence
Unites with its king!

The love that inflames me
For you, my conqueror
With its sweet ecstasy
Inundates my heart!

With the chorus (*con adore*):

Love, love, love to Jesus!

The girls, in the midst of clouds of incense, launch that supreme cry toward the heavens in loud and vibrant voices.

Then, in the profound silence of the prostrate, meditative crowd, the parrot, in a hoarse, cavernous, throaty voice, pronounces:

"Load of camels!"

There was a scandal, a general bewilderment; everyone had their noses in the air. The demoiselles of the congregation, to whom that insult was addressed, blushed, whispered and bit their lips. Monsieur le Curé raised his head indignantly toward the parrot, and, with the abruptness of the movement, his biretta fell off.

A child in the choir ran forward to pick it up, and placing his foot awkwardly on the steps of the altar, fell full length, ripping his red soutane.

The worthy priest, however, tried to pull himself together. In a rumbling stentorian tone he intoned: "*Tantum ergo . . .*"

"Load of camels! Load of camels! Load of camels!"

". . . *Sacramentum . . .*"

"Load of camels! Load of camels! Load of camels!"

The parrot was deafening; its plumage was bristling; it leaned forward as if it wanted to swoop down on the unfortunate chorists.

The curé continued, furiously: ". . . *Veneremur cernui . . .*"

"Load of camels! Load of camels! Load of camels!"

And while Monsieur Courgordon, his cranium bare, full

of wrath, furrowed his bushy russet eyebrows terribly and clenched his fists as if to strangle the impertinent beast, the tailor Paticlet, in the corridor opposite, was holding his belly with one hand and wiping his eyes with the other.

"No," he said to his comrade Houyon, "I'm laughing too much! I'll do myself an injury!"

And he continued writhing—to such an extent that when the procession had passed, it was necessary to untwist him.[1]

✳

As Montclar relived the memory of Lalie, the little brunette, his first, very confused amorous desire, blushing like a poppy under the coarse insults of the accused animal, Pépin des Grillons, amused by the recollection, added:

"I can still see the good curé standing up, furiously, taking hold of the monstrance, making a sign to the verger, and the procession moving off again, pursued by the parrot's cries. Do you remember, Patrice, it only shut up when the white dresses of the congregationists had disappeared on the far side of the Cours, under the plane trees . . ."

---

1 The second part of this sentence was added to the 1926 version, and does not appear in the 1885 version.

Pierrot and His Conscience

If you do not encounter fairies herein, good or bad, nor aerial sylphs, perhaps you can hear, as I have wished, the beating of a wounded heart?
Let us join hands.

Allegory

A young man went into a skull beneath an immense vault.

On the walls of that skull, frescoes painted by an artist—who has never existed down here—represented the passions: Love, Pride, Cupidity, Ambition, Lust, Gluttony and Sloth, attractive and smiling; Jealousy, Anger and Envy, jaundiced and grim. The daylight was coming from below via the cavernous eyes, whose two round windows allowed the sunlight to penetrate and the passers-by, the trees and the sidewalks outside to be seen.

Other pale young men entered in black suits, some of whom sat down on benches placed in a hemicycle; and others, standing up, strolled through the cranium. With a gnawing passion, or several, in the depths of their hearts, they chatted soundlessly and laughed joylessly.

Soon, an alma arrived, dressed in mourning, tightly

enclosed in her supple dress, like an Egyptian mummy in its bandages. She looked at each of them, and seemed to be intimately acquainted with them all.

The young man wanted to know who the alma was, who also resembled his mistress. He asked a circulating dung beetle: "What is her name?"

"Dolor: an unfashionable woman."

I

On the stroke of eleven o'clock, at Mid-Lent, Pierrot woke up in his coffin in the middle of Montmartre cemetery—for he had wanted to be buried in a Parisian location, at the foot of the inspiring hill. What humus of the dead is more alive than that?

Pére-Lachaise is asleep in an undistinguished faubourg. At the very most, at rare intervals, the dead hear the blade of the guillotine in the Place de la Roquette cutting off the freshly shaven head of a murderer. Montparnasse Cemetery, near as it may be to the Rue de la Gaité, is equally sad, because of its distance from the Opéra and the Varietés. The dead of Montparnasse cemetery are obliged to take the omnibus to come to the great boulevards, and even then they have to change.

As for Clamart, it is Cayenne.

Pierrot had not wanted to rest in a cemetery of exiles. He had amused himself once and had led a life of electric speed, so successfully that he had been worn out at thirty. But from his leaden coffin at Montmartre—in the family vault of the Pierrots, his ancestors—he perceived the sounds of the festival, gusts of the music of the ball, weary refrains of the carnival, grey rhythms of waltzes, strident blasts of brass, attenuated in passing through the crêpe of the night, or the moaning of violins, and the fatigued laughter of the celebrants.

A few steps away, so to speak, are the great joyous halls of Montmartre; a few paces further on, the Opéra, where Métra and Fahrbach—or at least their specters—were directing their orchestras on the night of the last masked ball.[1]

In the coffin, between the ill-joined planks—do re mi te . . . mi mi do do . . . mi mi . . . mi mi—the white and the black, the crotchets, quavers, semiquavers and demisemiquavers entered like caresses, sonorous straws carried by the wind, dying folderols, soothing echoes of everlasting themes, shreds of crazy trills and the languorous waltz: "Come with me to hail the spring."

The uncertain roses, the ungraspable lilacs and the violets of dreams smelled sweet; a mysterious April blew warm and intoxicating breezes; the phallic fauns were running, singing, seeking kisses, and the faunesses were whispering in the shade of the tender green foliage of woods as imprecise as dreams. The waves were unfurling softly with a quasi-sensual plaint; on the beaches, the sirens veiled in the fluid gauze of the surf, in the incessantly fleeing forms of the water, were calling.

Waltzes were whispering their enervating rhythms in Pierrot's ears—mi mi, do do, mi mi—in the dream of his awakening; he soon got up, and his Conscience got up with him.

---

1 Olivier Métra (1830-1889), a composer best known for his waltzes, was, at various times, the orchestra-leader at the Bal Mabile and the Folies Bergères. Philipp Fahrbach Jr. (1843-1895) performed frequently in Paris in the 1870s and 1880s with the orchestra he took over from his father Philipp Fahrbach Sr. (1815-1885); both were prolific composers of dance music.

II

They emerged from the vault, the key to which Pierrot had in his pocket, and, without following the streets of the dead, gliding between the funerary monuments, bumping into crosses and skimming the grass, they went forth arm in arm to see whether the fast set of the Parisian Mid-Lent still existed.

Pierrot had loved countless women—or, if he had not loved them all, he had done with them what one does when one is loved. He had known virgins who did not want to be virgins any longer, married women for whom Monsieur Joseph Prudhomme was no longer sufficient, pretty girls who, in spite of their carmined and merchandised lips, had adored him, since they had only ruined his health. He had been summoned by bailiffs to appointments he had never kept, and moneylenders had regretted his death, because they had lost before that flight all hope of being repaid when Pierrot settled down. And Pierrot was all white, with his cream silk costume with large buttons, his powdered face, his headscarf and his hat pointing at the stars—but his Conscience was all black.

Her name was Pierrette, and, doubtless, for that night, Carêmette. She was as similar—exquisitely so, delicately androgynous in womanly form—to her comrade as a drop of ink is to a drop of water, with her whimsical costume: short black satin culottes, a black collarette and a transparent black bodice, low-cut and slit to the waist, forming a delightful frame for her white bosom and her small up-turned breasts, black silk stockings and black gloves. She was black, save for the face, as fresh and clear as could ever be seen, pink or white, so young and so elegant, in her ingenuous flesh—for that Conscience might have been black, but she never showed it, and always had that pretty face; she was black because of her friend's vices, but she did not hold that against him, and the Conscience walked in Pierrot's company like a sister.

She had consented to her brother's transient amours and still lent herself to this posthumous curiosity.

After having themselves painted by a Montmartran art student, on two extravagant cards, suspended around their necks, one by a white ribbon and the other by a black one, they crossed the Boulevard de Batignolles and soon went around the sails of the windmill, like wings of fire, purple and gold:

> *Perched on the high hill,*
> *coiffed with a pointed hat,*
> *the windmill makes white flour*
> *of the virtue of young women.*

II

Pierrot and his Conscience went into the flamboyant and iridescent hall, decked with the flags of all nations— money has no fatherland—and where, to the hectic racket of dance music, female flesh was traded, but they did not stay long. No one there was joyful. The Desdemonas, the Juliets and the Chimènes—none clad in tights, their legs brilliant with silk—were parading there, offering their lips to anyone, flirting with messieurs good for three or five louis. Not even striving for hilarity, bored males were circulating.

Six English girls, who had been applauded furiously a few minutes before, three dressed as boys and three as androgynous dancers, were now among the crowd again, stroked incessantly by gross desires: six English scamps in red silk skirts and black stockings, their faces impassive, simultaneously perverse and naïve, dancing an extraordinary jig; two were clad in the simple blue dresses of the Salvation Army, coiffed with the large winged funnel-shaped hats of novice evangelists. A man, their nominal father, in a sea-green jersey on which was inscribed in yellow letters: *Salutation Army: Love One Another*, was leading that little family Saturnalia, his entire body writhing and his face phlegmatic.

Ohé, the vices! Ohé, the depraved! You who love women, they were three little girls yesterday. Ohé, you who are weary of the age-old normal gestures, their sisters are three boys.

Further away, in the middle of a quintuple circle of men, four dancers—one of whom, a woodlouse, is beginning to be famous and is already the center of attention of all gazes—were leaping and prancing in a thicket of lace in which the sex, for alert eyes, could occasionally be glimpsed. The four girls were engaged in a dialogue, with thrusts of the hips, lewd contortions, waddling stances and indecent steps that quivered before ecstatic drunkards, sometimes removing their hats.

As they passed through the host of exhibits, Pierrot and his Conscience heard scraps of conversations. A whore demanded of an old man whether "corridor" is written with two /s; the old man replied that it is generally pronounced with two /s but always written with two rs.[1]

In one corner, people were talking about the rise in rents.

One besuited man said to another: "What does Chose live on?"

The other replied: "He was rich once."

A vicious and mystical girl, playing with a fan, almost naked in a straight transparent dress imprinted with daises, with a holy aureole attached to a russet chignon, cleaved through a group of men. "For whom is the wife of Saint Louis?" she asked.

"For me," replied the majority of the males.

"For all!" she replied.

And she planted herself in front of those she thought were "serious."

Everyone, at that masked ball, was preoccupied with money, the women with earning it, the men with not spending it.

A blonde, naked in a clear sheath beneath an ash-gray tulle skirt speckled with stars, was cynically carrying a sign in her hand saying: ROOM TO LET.

Someone asked: "At the front?"

With the ingenuous smile of a virgin in May-blossom time, she replied: "Yes, but I also have a small apartment at the back."

"How much?"

They haggled.

Quickly, Pierrot and his Conscience left in a fiacre for the Opéra.

---

1 The pun, likening a *corridor* to a place where people bump into one another, translates straightforwardly.

On the sidewalk, two men in overcoats, at least one of whom should have had a tricorn hat, were quarreling.

"I'm not in competition with you."

"Why not?"

"It would be a naval combat."

In the flamboyant and iridescent hall, decked in the flags of all nations—money and pleasure have no fatherland—hectic dance music was blaring; the Eves, the Juliets, the Rodrigues, the Chimènes and the Agnèses, on offer at reduced prices or to the highest bidder, were parading provocative gazes beneath painted eyelashes, all mouths promising, while bored males circulated, not even striving for hilarity.

IV

The present was too improper and repugnant. The coach-man descended toward the great boulevards at a gallop. Quarter past midnight. Seeing the tranquil streets, with scarce passers-by, the two dead individuals recalled the era when, every year, the escaped carnival precipitated, via all the streets neighboring the Opéra, delirious, capricious, amorous, infernal and disheveled, into the overflow-ing cafés, ballrooms and night-restaurants. They evoked memories on the way.

The Conscience said to Pierrot: "We've done well to die, since laughter is dead, replaced by sniggering. Dead too is the need to love! Dead is whimsy, dead caprice, dead the passions—save for the bitter desire for wealth—dead is joy! We, the deceased, are the more joyful, for, in our coffin, and now, in this other 'pine box,' we're awakening remembrance . . .

"Have you forgotten, Pierrot, the blonde Musette who cherished you in the Latin Quarter? When you close your eyes, do you see again the Zerbinette, whom you encountered one evening at the Opera Ball in the Rue Le Peletier, who adored you for an entire summer? You loved the boating trips in the cheerful sunlight on the Marne; while, sitting in the prow, she let her dangling legs trail her bare feet in the water, you improvised a poem in *terza rima* for her:

> *Beauty, your arms are pale, your laughter silvery.*
> *Raise your satin skirt up higher for me,*
> *Show the flesh that has the soft shades of morning.*

"There was a hiatus; after which—oh, the lovely viewpoint!—Zerbinette raised her dress. The banks were bordered with willows, whose supple branches swayed overhead. No one could see you. I, your Conscience, was there; but I did not reproach you for anything, because you were twenty years old."

V

The fiacre arrived at the Opéra, inundated with electric light, before which policemen and Republican Guards— one might have thought the latter, stiff and superb in the saddle, polychromatic living statues—contained a thousand obstinate idlers on the sidewalk, having cleared a void. Hundreds of fiacres and coupés were thus traversing the square, stopping at the foot of the grand façade. But several carriages stopped further away, discreetly, under the subscribers' peristyle.

Oh, the multicolored pell-mell of the carnival, climbing the steps, hastening toward the doors! Oh, here and there, the pretty profiles under silken hoods and somber masks in which the eyes scintillated more, while the mouth smiled, excited, by the cold and a hope of pleasure, with a more vivid influx of blood! Oh, all of that, the seigneurs with equivocal clothing, the rejected doublets, the Tabarins, the urchinettes, the clowns, the soubrettes, the girlish tribe, the tucked-up and the half-dressed, the Zerbinettes, and then the cocadrilles, the Giangurgolos, the legendary disguises, fantasies and extravagances, dominos of every kind, a fearful population, curious bourgeois on family excursions and wild sprees, behaving like hooligans, a tide of tuxedos! All of that—Paris embarked for Cythera and Lesbos, for here and there, for far away, for elsewhere—departed, nostrils vibrant, in quest of amour, of kisses, of Pleasure.

Pierrot and his Conscience climbed the steps leading to the vestibule. They had nothing to leave in the cloakroom, and the attendants looked glum. Black suits, standing on the monumental stairway, watched the newcomers, especially the women; they watched, without finding a flash of wit, while masked splenetic individuals wove spider-webs in their heads; they watched.

And nothing more.

One of them, Trésel, the young Duc, seized from behind, with both hands, lewdly, a woman who face was hidden by a thick mantilla of triple lace, and whose forms were plump. She turned round, looked the insolent fellow up and down, to judge whether or not she ought to forgive him, and said, scornfully: "You're not handsome enough to be so bold." As the simpleton looked at her, smugly, she went on: "Don't you know the proverb: to the innocent, full hands?"

Pierrot white and Pierrot black had a sensational passage through the corridors of the boxes, amid the ebony jackets, the satin dominos and veiled women, and a few other masks. Fahrbach, slender and blond—if it wasn't him it should have been—near the foyer, with a few attentive groups of music-lovers of melomaniacs around his orchestra, was playing a piece with shrill and staccato rhythms, which sometimes seemed to be traversed by the wingbeats of a flock of storks.

VI

Finally, Pierrot white and Pierrot black penetrated into the hall opposite the orchestra by means of a broad, straight stairway garnished with municipal guards and standard lamps, at the foot of which bursts of instruments, by virtue of a baroque acoustic effect of the monument, came to die like waves.

The crowd was there, which drew the two companions away.

Above the sparkling gamut of that violet, indigo, black, green, yellow, orange and red crowd; above the plumes of all colors, tricorn hats and lustrine dominos, loose or tight, toques, sombreros and stovepipe hats; above the women clad as huntresses, with bows and quivers, soldiers, marvels of the Directoire, rag-pickers and seigneurs of the time of Louis XIV or the genteel century, Matamores, Scapins, shepherdesses—who had often seen the wolf—Eves still tempting with the forbidden fruits of the lost paradise;

above the beadles, the Spanish students with their guitars and spoons, eunuchs, tuxedos, pierrots, pierrettes, little cicadas—the patron saint of poets, "Saint Cicada, pray for us"; above the harlequins with their bats, harlequines, clownesses, spindly legs, sculpted rumps, Lulus, Polichinelles with their humps, Clodoches, Columbines, débardeurs, toreros, Robert Macaires and Bertrands, alguazils, cranes with babies, Muscadines and Rigolboches; above the paid masks and a thousand black suits, playing the fool there as elsewhere; above the yawns, quips and laughter, the bacchanal, the sabbat and the epileptic commotion, feet and calves in the air, and in the still-light atmosphere, moist armpits; above the dislocated capering and leaping, Olivier, the poet of Roses, of bewitching waves of eternal tumult, blue waves in which the emerald of wrack winds in serpentine fashion—the poet of fauns calling in the thickets—is guiding the decadence of the carnival, his head turned to the right, his face pensive and placid, hair curly and as if powdered, moustache feline, melancholy eyes seemingly staring at an imaginary jester, who, on the edge of a front-of-stage box reminiscent of a cenotaph, is doubtless expiring, tipped backwards, still shaking his bells one last time.

Métra, the musician of Roses, of pink roses, white roses, roses, and svelte women, or his appearance, his memory returned, is profiled, bow in hand, behind his music stand, his tall, elegant silhouette making melodious poetry flow from violins and brass instruments.

The variegated swarming crowd of sworn masks waltzed, in a mist of gas and dust, contemplated by dazed black suits and by the ladies and gentleman of boxes, afflicted by ennui. In some, however, people were enjoying

41

themselves. Dominos harpooned in the vast, slightly mysterious corridors and at the top of the great stairway, and veiled women that were almost violated in order to test the quality of the merchandise, suddenly pushed from the depths of boxes, uttered little squeals.

In two or three boxes, were there perhaps, masked aristocratic ladies, awaited in anxiety and ardently cherished, becoming infatuated? In others—those of the worldly clubs and princes of the fête—there was a pretty coming-and-going of elegant ladies, not always guaranteed distinguished, and of friends, while, higher up, doubtless, others of both sexes, no longer hearing the echoes of waltzes, polkas and quadrilles, the monotonous buzz of a sensual rumor, far from municipal guards, were in paradise, the abode of the blessed.

Métra, or his shade, with his bow, led all these things.

Musard,[1] face pockmarked, was livid and funereal, almost macabre, in the midst of joyous fools who sometimes carried him in triumph. Strauss seemed an unostentatious bourgeois lost in bad and bellowing company. Arban,[2] features fixed, with side-whiskers, in the phlegmatic appearance of a millionaire's butler, maintained an impassive correction; Fahrbach, blue-eyed, pensive before the audience—why are those who create or unleash joy almost always melancholy?

Quite indifferent to the chaos of the dance, was Métra, who seemed drowsy in the midst of a furious rush to pleasure—or at least the attempt—thinking that after this

---

1 Philippe Musard (1792-1859), long before Champsaur's time, had been famous, like Olivier Métra, as an orchestra-leader at Parisian balls.
2 The conductor and composer Jean-Baptiste Arban (1825-1889).

Mid-Lent, spring would soon arrive, with his companion, April?

Still the black suits were massed in admiration in the hall, in the sparkling furnace, before hundred-sou costumes. Here and there, nevertheless, were masks for caprice, and some were genteel—but they were counted. There was, for example, a rabbit carrying a carrot from which, at moment, a doll surged, with a rounded hat, furious with the rabbit. Another, insolent in laughter and prettiness, was shooting at pigeons. Another, bare-armed, with a fresh mouth, was a queen of hearts, with hearts sewn over her gown and the motto *There are enough for everyone* standing out in golden letters from the loose belt. A former actress, dressed up as Figaro, was repeating from time to time: "I still sharpen my pen and ask someone . . ."

A brunette woman without a mask, with short hair, supple and Tanagrian in a black suit, had her arm around the waist of a blonde, veiled girl-friend in a mauve domino, and their smitten duo—with an effrontery and charming indecency careless of what anyone might say—smiled at the curious and slightly troubled gazes that greeted them in passing.

To one bourgeois group, the men rather fat and the women somewhat out-of-date, who applauded them ironically, the short-haired brunette cried: "Thank you, worthy people." And as she drew the mauve domino away, she hurled at them: "May God protect your daughters from ours!"

The blonde girl-friend, with hectic curls over her nape, spirited and frisky, burst out laughing, and her laughter rippled beneath a quadruple beard of lace.

VII

A petite woman, lightly clad as a dragonfly in a blue silk leotard, with azure wings that scintillated behind her shoulders, appetizing and full of verve, her mouth fresh, insinuated herself into groups, among the thickets of colors, the tumult of accoutrements, in quest of a fop who would pay for her gauzy wings and her supper.

Excessive paradoxes, life at full tilt, a sabbat, a gallop, a chamade, gaiety to the point of paroxysm, pleasure flat out, would you believe it, my dear? Shall we have supper? Shall we not have supper?

It is the fair of amours.

The remainder—what remainder?—was composed of trivia, a salmagundi of obsolete, tasteless masks, theatrical cast-offs. The little blonde dragonfly was chatting with a glow-worm who was saying stupid things. The dragonfly, exciting and impish, was making fun of him, and said, pointing to his extinct lantern: "It's not enough, my little glow-worm, to have a tail; it's also necessary for it to light up."

VIII

At intervals, lovely legs passed by, nacreous in silk stockings, the beautiful bare shoulders and delicious necks of women. There, a woman in Mercure Galante said to a carnival Turk with bouffant trousers, his head coiffed by a fez, that people who wear skullcaps deserve them.

Pierrot black, meanwhile—the Conscience—in her vibrant voice, was sounding a wake-up call of memories to Pierrot white, more blanched than ever, claiming that the ball had the air of a burial. Agitating the flaps of her overly long sleeves at the extremities of his hands, she cried:

"Where are the jesters of old? Where is the society of Gavarni?[1] Our epoch is too sage. Where is the orchestra-leader accompanying the infernal gallop passing like a whirlwind? There are idlers who can say nothing but *gaga, Maman* and *twenty-five louis* and tell one another that they've come from some gambling den where they held a bank and suffered heavy losses . . .

"Those who work, by necessity, have to be anxious about their future. The young, devoid of belief, devoid of amour, devoid of ideals, and tormented by the sole obsession of rapid gain, are not young, and do not have on their lips and in their eyes the song of their twenty years. They no longer dance. The anxiety of money harasses them, because money has become King and God. Old men can be seen who smile more than these faded or aborted youths. They come to the ball with their senses chilled and hearts empty, in order to have come, to tell others that they have come, because they hoped—these individuals exhausted by life, or simply exhausted, who claim, O irony, to be living fast—to kill ennui more noisily here, but also more bleakly, more easily than elsewhere; others because they hoped to meet someone and 'have an affair.'

---

1 The illustrator who signed his work Paul Gavarni (Sulpice-Guillaume Chevalier, 1804-1866) did most of his later work for the humorous periodical *Le Charivari*, where he provided a running pictorial chronicle of Parisian high life.

"Where is Théo who sported a red waistcoat?[1] Where is Lord Seymour?[2] Arsouille? Caderousse and Prince Citron?[3] Where are the true fast livers, the reckless? All dead . . .

"And the women of the world? Do they even still exist? They've been replaced by rich women. Where are the intrigues, the imbroglios, the mysteries? Only the gibes remain. No more great courtesans, even, but on the other hand, petty whores are flourishing."

A young man who had an orchid in his buttonhole and was walking, top hat in hand, behind the two comrades, now grave, had heard Pierrot black's elegy. He interrupted her.

"Conscience, you would do better to sell yourself."

Disdainful, she did not reply, and continued her plaint.

"I, your Conscience, Pierrot, regret Gavarni's sluts, the masks inspired by Daumier; I regret the insensate, the dreamers, the spendthrifts of fortunes and the spendthrifts of the future . . ."

"Not good, that! No, not modern! Not twilight of the century," interjected the young man who was still marching on their heels.

---

1 Théophile Gautier famously wore a red waistcoat at the première of Victor Hugo's *Hernani* in 1830.

2 Probably Richard Seymour-Conway, fourth Marquess of Hertford (1800-1870), who owned a town house in Paris and the Château de Bagatelle in the Bois de Boulogne.

3 Arsouille is a generic term for louche debauchees. "Prince Citron" was the nickname of William, Prince of Orange (1840-1879), who notoriously followed such a lifestyle while in exile in Paris, until it killed him; the nickname, taken up by the newspapers who reported the Prince's antics, was bestowed on him by his companion in debauchery, the Duc de Gramont-Caderousse.

"I regret," she continued, without paying any heed to that reasonable sarcasm, "the aristocratic courtesans, I hate the whores and I weep for dead youth . . ."

IX

Pierrot white murmured softly to Pierrot black that doubtless their youth alone had expired, since the dead were elsewhere, and he directed the Conscience's attention to another petite woman, marvelously decked out in violet and perfumed with the floral essence. Beside her were marching, in single file, thirty gentlemen in gold. They represented bankers. Their opera hats were covered with gold paper, and their frock coats, trousers, waistcoats and shoes were also gold, although their gloves and cravats were white. They were all very correct and very elegant. They were grave and sad, cutting through groups of masks and black suits. Their golden file marked the pecuniary note of modern society. Each of them was Gold, a mute and powerful individual, worth as much as talent and nobility.

Pierrot white and Pierrot black applauded their passage.

The last of the gentlemen in gold detached himself from the chaplet and came toward the two Pierrots.

"You must be two brothers . . ." He read the card that the two of them silently held out to him. "Oh! You're only One! I beg your pardon; I hadn't realized. The clown Pierrot, duplicated, with his Conscience . . . Do you know that not all humans would be delighted if their personality could be thus divided and their soul shown to them? It would often be blacker than yours, Pierrot. She's black, your Conscience, but she's agreeable . . . very agreeable.

47

Nigra sed formosa, like the Shulamite of the canticle.[1] That's all right! You seem to be having a good time here, for the disinterred . . .

"Eh! Look at that red Polichinelle. Even her face is vermilion. It's as crimson as you're white, and you're black . . ." He took Pierrot white by the arm to one side, and Pierrot black to the other, and drew them away. "Let's go have a bottle of champagne at the buffet. Her adventure will be told to you. It's me who's inviting you, because I'm gold . . . or at least gold plate . . ."

Pierrot white, Pierror black and the golden gentleman escaped from the hall, where the atmosphere was becoming noxious, the saline odors of flesh becoming too strong, and through one of the subterranean passages that are underneath the proscenium to either side, they went into the corridor of the boxes, where, following the initial pursuits of lovers of the upper crust, silk dominos and pretty or ugly women of a common stripe in lace mantillas were now strolling. Along the walls, black suits were standing like rows of onions, between which contrary currents were passing of other black suits and young women.

An admirable woman of loose morals, disguised as Zanetto,[2] with a worn velvet mantle attached to her shoulder and falling all the way to the ground, was repeating in a caressant tone the unique line:

---

1 The source quotation from the *Song of Songs* is *Nigra sum sed formosa* [I am black and beautiful]; it was frequently attached as a device to images of the Black Madonna.

2 Presumably the character in Goldoni's comedy known in English as *The Venetian Twins*; it cannot be the minstrel in Mascagni's 1896 opera of that title, which had not yet reached Paris when the story was published.

Give me money, for I love my mother.

In vulgar prose, she added that she was indeed "working" for her mother, who had just give birth to her thirteenth child.

"The first of the second dozen," someone remarked, a monocled boulevardier.

Further away a woman sighing amorously, clad as a centauress, with superb plump arms, bare save for gloves that came up to the elbow, was delightful. Her corset—a breastplate in fine steel sequins, lightly woven, of minuscule design, meekly following her contours—with a very low neckline as broad as a finger over the shoulder, tightly laced in an imperceptible manner, molded an admirable figure, supple and undulating, with serpentine movements, and the undersides of semi-naked breasts that surged forth therefrom. Her flesh-colored tights bore a silver horseshoe at the intersection. Oh, a magnificent beast, with her black hair, silky at the nape, falling in an equine tail to the tips of her cothurnes, her entire splendid being having the integrity of forms engendered in a perfect successive harmony, by both components. Leaning back over the arm of a fat gentleman, she simulated palpitation. Putting her weight on one leg, extending the other in an exceedingly chic pose, she said:

"Are there many women here whose lines are so pure? And it's all similar"—with a gesture of ingenuous vice she pointed at the troubling jewel. "How much will you give me for my horseshoe?"

She put her foot down, on the heel of which a little silver bell rang, and, swooning, her eyes white, leaned her head on the shoulder of the fat gentleman.

He declared that a woman like that was worth two thousand a month, and asked six of his friends if they wanted to go into partnership with him, each having one day a week.

"So be it," she said, "and for your good idea, old fellow, you can have Sunday, the chic day."

X

In the corridors, the exhausted and depressed were collapsing on benches, or even on the stone balustrade at the top of the staircase. The curious were peering through the windows of boxes.

In a group of men gathered around a fisherwoman catching her death of cold in a bathing costume, Pierrot and his Conscience perceived a banker—or acrobat— who they had once known before their death, and who had already possessed a capital of six million and debts of three million, which makes nine.

Sometimes, there was pushing in the vicinity of the boxes. Near Fahrbach's orchestra, as they were about to go into the buffet, they heard a fragment of an argument:

"You've sold your wife."

"So have you."

"But I went bankrupt."

He had trafficked his wife, but had not delivered her. That was cleverer. Pierrot white and Pierrot back exchanged sad smiles, but the gentleman in gold remained impassive, for evidently a woman, even married, is a negotiable animal, provided that one does not break the code—although one can get around it.

They sat down in the gallery, which makes an angle with the foyer, from which they could hear the strange airs of Fahrbach, the plaintive scraping of cellos. A grasshopper in a muslin beret atop bright chestnut hair, a sea-green dress and long wings of the same hue, with silvery tips, had come in quest of a glass of champagne.

Then the gentleman in gold commenced, as promised, the story of the red Polichinelle.

"There was once a husband who, wanting to go to the Opéra Ball to have a little fun, ordered a red Polichinelle costume from his tailor. His wife, however, suspected a deceit—just between us, she had found a letter from the tailor asking him if he wanted a fine Polichinelle hump or only half a hump; Madame had the deplorable habit of rummaging through Monsieur's affairs—so she decided to catch him in the knavery and make him expiate it. For that purpose, she resolved to go to the Opéra Ball too, and she bought a symbolic yellow domino, her husband's future colors. But the husband chanced to catch a glimpse of the yellow domino, and thought of a possible treason on his wife's part, thinking that he was not under suspicion. Both of them, therefore, came to the last ball.

"At half past midnight, a red Polichinelle arrives. He encounters, in the corridor of the boxes, the buttercup domino. The Polichinelle flirts with the domino. That goes very smoothly, as if on castors. One goes very quickly on castors to the divan . . .

"Naturally, the couple were masked, and it's also necessary to say that they had both disguised their voices . . .

"The lady allows herself to be drawn away, at one o'clock in the morning, to a private room. Although they have always remained veiled, they have not remained decent. Oh no! No need to pretend any longer, is there? Suddenly, the red Polichinelle snatches away the yellow domino's mask, and the yellow domino removes the red Polichinelle's mask, crying: 'Ah! You lead a Polichinelle's life! You pay for a whole hump, half isn't sufficient . . .' She stops dead. 'You're not my husband!'

"And he, stamping his feet with joy, says: 'We're going to have some fun! You're not my wife!'

"Yes, little Pierrot, and you, dear Madame, it was neither one of them!"

The gentleman in gold got up in order to rejoin the file of bankers, who were passing again, this time followed by a file of pretty girls smitten with them; but, perceiving a red Polichinelle all alone, he added that that must be the husband whose wife had been foraged, at the last Opéra Ball, by another red Polichinelle, unless it was a third husband.

"Oh, the life of Polichinelle!" said the gentleman in gold to the red hump wandering alone.

"The advice of Polichinelle is not to care about anything, even gold."

"Not possible, that," said a petite woman disguised as Scottish hospitality.

XI

It was the time when suppers were organized. People went to them two by two, each man with his lady companion, or in groups. A few dancers, bit-part players in theaters, and a few dancing girls, rejected prostitutes, fatigued, were beginning to invade the corridors and the foyer.

Oh, all of that, the seigneurs with equivocal clothing, the rejected doublets, the Tabarins, the urchinettes, the clowns, the soubrettes, the girlish tribe, the tucked-up and the half-dressed, the Zerbinettes, and then the cocadrilles, the Giangurgolos, the legendary disguises, fantasies and extravagances, dominos of every kind, a fearful population, curious bourgeois on family excursions and wild sprees, behaving like hooligans, the tide of tuxedos! All of that—Paris embarked for Cythera and Lesbos, for here and there, for far away, for elsewhere—which, before midnight, departed, nostrils vibrant, in quest of amour, of kisses, of Pleasure! Shall we have supper? Shall we not have supper?

Waltzes, dying folderols, lulling echoes of obsessive refrains, shreds of crazy trills, waltzes agonizing among the violet, indigo, black, green, yellow, orange, red crowd, dominos of lustrine or silk, sombreros, stovepipe hats, Spanish students, pierrots, pierrettes, harlequines, clownesses, polichinelles, muscadines—waltzes whispered beyond the laughter, the bacchanal. And in the corridors, women were still being violated.

But the tuxedos were beginning to slip away.

Meanwhile, the thirty gentlemen in gold suits, still in single file, followed by women in dominos, ball gowns and tights, also assembled in single file behind them by the omnipotence of gold, were making a tour of Fahrbach's orchestra, which was playing the maestro's popular waltz, *Tout à la joie,*[1] while one of the last tuxedos, putting his gloved hands to his mouth, shouted from the top of the staircase to the picturesque file that was moving

---

1 Philippe Fahrbach Jr.'s *"Tout à la joie!"* is actually a polka.

away: "Who wants to sup with someone who's bored to death?"

A fop collapsed on the balcony, paralyzed on the stone balustrade, suddenly sprang into action and clamored in reply, dominating the orchestra's whirlwind of joy with the knell of his dolorous voice: "Brother, it's necessary to die!"

In the clement penumbra of the corridors, here and there, in the crowd, there are old men's quips, obscene whispers, bursts of nervous laughter, crude words, bold caresses, the exasperated aroma of women, fever, ennui, torpor, and the sudden brutal pressure of black-suited boors upon a young woman lifted up by thirty lubricious hands, who, legs akimbo, quivering in mid-air, struggles horizontally above a drunken circle of carters in frock-coats; all the arms converge toward an invisible point. For a moment, there in an indescribable clutching, a swarming stupor; then a scream of terror, and the rosy flash of a little naked thigh in the frisson of a lifted dress, beneath which lacy underwear is sought, and torn away in order to reach the objective.

Pierrot white and Pierrot black, sickened by that coarse dementia, of an almost silent lust—oh, the urchins, the gay dogs, the good-time girls, the balochards, débardeurs and débardeuses of Gavarni,[1] the witty heroes, the defunct heroes of the carnivals of old!—released the grasshopper, not finding on her lips, as if faded by wear and tear, on which one suspected the traces of an army of paying

1 Gavarni played a considerable part in popularizing the stereotypes of the *balochard*, a dance-hall musician, and the *débardeur*, literally a dock-worker, although the term took on a second life as a standardized masked-ball costume modelled on the illustrator's caricature.

kisses, the ideal imagined for the night, the fantastic night for which they have escaped the tomb.

Suddenly, before them, a lovely silhouette appeared of a slim woman with ardent, coppery red hair, with a black mask, an exceedingly low-cut sheath dress and very long black gloves, only allowing the sight of the troubling summits of bare arms. A gentleman in a black suit, florid with a cattleya, prostrate at the woman's knees, his left hand holding his opera hat against the floor, seemed to be murmuring a canticle of feigned adoration.

After examining him carefully, she darted: "Yes, the chic but not the check."

Then she took the arm of a gentleman in gold, with the head of a calf, who was passing.

Around, everywhere, here and there, young women were hastening, anxious to find a supper, and the rest. Drunkards were making a semblance of laughter.

Here, a gypsy, with the lascivious roll of a belly dance, is making a belt of sequins tinkle over her hips. There, a violet domino, a Cytherean bishop *in partibus*, in the corner of a corridor, her foot on a bench, with an abrupt tug, as if to pull up her silk stocking over her elegant leg—the flick of a garter—shows a little bare flesh; her amorous feline eyes shine and appeal.

Further away, there were darted tongues, thrusts of fans, laughter, promises and refusals that meant yes.

Here, again, in the penumbra of the corridor of the amphitheater, childish jostling, the audacities of invisible hands under dresses, from in front or behind, in the crowd, the squeals of recalcitrant dominos, curious silences; further away, stupefaction, the base joy of the great hall, in which the multicolored tawdry finery is swarming, from which human odors rise up. And everywhere, the bargaining is becoming more urgent.

A frail blonde, very thin, disguised as a jockey, radiating youth, advances: "Would you like a little 'tip?' Monsieur?"

Pierrot and his Conscience went downstairs.

Outside the cloakroom, a woman in tights, having put on her fur coat, parted it and, teasingly, almost naked against the dark furry backcloth, said: "Would you like to nestle in my fur, my dear Pierrot. There's plenty of room for you, you see."

Her eyes were blue: the pale blue of banknotes.

XII

Pierrot was all white, with his costume in cream silk, with large buttons, his powdered face, his chin-strap and his hat pointing toward the stars. But his Conscience was all black, suggestive, so exquisitely and delicately androgynous, although female, of his counterpart, like a drop of ink to a drop of water; with her fantastic costume, culottes of black satin, a black collarette and a transparent black bodice, split to the waist, forming a delightful frame for the white bosom and the small high-pointed breasts, black silk stockings and black gloves.

She was black—save for the face, as fresh and bright as what could be seen, pink or white, so young and so elegant, or her ingenuous flesh; for a Conscience might be black, but never shows herself as such, and always has a pretty face. She was black because of her friend's vices, but she never held that against him, and the Conscience walked in Pierrot's company like a sister . . .

Without listening, without seeing, they went out on to the boulevard. In the corner of the square and the Boulevard des Capucines, the advertisement for the masked ball at the Opéra was still flamboyant, in gaslit letters; a crowd had gathered there.

Pierrot and his Conscience perceived a slender, supremely aristocratic woman. Entirely dressed in black, as tight and slim in her dress as a sword in its sheath, she had a marvelous fleece of hair the color of pale ale, and on that tawny hair, which fell over her neck in a bushy tangle, was a broad-brimmed black hat on which a bloody dead owl had subsided. One might have thought that it represented the wisdom of that strange and mysterious woman.

A lace veil descended from the hat over the face, but through its cobweb mesh shone two diabolical eyes. Her entire being emitted a bizarre charm, compounded of a mixture of chastity and vice, of distinguished flesh and vulgar savor, or virginal ingenuousness and two fine mortal sins, pride and lust.

Passers-by arranged themselves in two ranks to let the veiled unknown pass.

A ragpicker in his forties, an unlucky bachelor, leaving his work momentarily to idle and watch the people trying to have fun, a difficult métier, admired her with eyes full of desire and stupor. For a long time—two years—he had not been able to reward himself with a suitable woman, for he did not debase himself, because of the parchment he had once received.

The poor devil, caressing the handle of his hook angrily, muttered:

"And yet, I . . ."

She only heard the last word; even stiffer than the stick the rag-picker showed her, she turned her head toward him for a second, scornful and flattered.

Where had she come from? She had not been seen at the ball. Was she in a box? Why was she alone? Had she fallen to the boulevard from one of the stars that were scintillating in the sky in thousands?

Where was she going, so elegant and fine? Where was that slenderness going, whose eyes, beneath the veil, sometimes had the coruscation of two stars?

The Eyes were extraordinary. It seemed at first that they communicated vertigo to whomever they settled upon: tempting Eyes, voluptuous Eyes, tender and deceitful, the Eyes of an enchantress whose irises shone like two emeralds. Sometimes, you might have thought that they brushed you, those Eyes of a magicienne and a demoniac, with a plaintive gaze, seductive with light and softness; sometimes, despotic, striped with gold, spangled with sparks, they were infinite gardens of strange, venomous flowers blossoming in their purity.

Their gleams were magnetic.

XIII

Pierrot white advanced toward Her. With a foolish aplomb, his arm reached round the supple waist, the hand gripping.

"This one," he said, "must be more intelligent than the others."

After a sudden and instinctive corporeal rebellion, the unknown woman stared at the audacious individual; then, only resisting the enveloping arm to the extent necessary for a charming modesty, she said: "No, I'm stupid."

"Let's chat, then."

"All right. You can sustain your intelligence, and I my stupidity."

"Do you belong to the salon, or the theater?"

"No, I belong to the street."

Then, with an affectation of infinite politeness he offered his arm; she accepted. The fantasist started talking amorously, for he sensed a fluid intoxicating him, escaped from and incessantly emitted by the dainty gloved hand he was supporting, conquering him entirely, convincing him that She realized his feminine ideal.

She listened, always replying to his enthusiasms with skeptical and droll responses.

Pierrot chatted, seeking the words in his heart, and she in her mind.

The Conscience walked behind holding the train of her dress, for, in moments of amorous intoxication, Conscience often becomes humble and cowardly. Nevertheless, she whispered softly in her friend's ear:

"Be careful, Pierrot. She's one of those exquisitely artificial women, painted and powdered, deliciously dressed and costumed, too pretty, more beautiful in appearance than is natural . . ."

"So what?"

"When unwrapped, there's nothing underneath."

Pierror white paid no heed to the observation of his Conscience. He took the unknown woman to a private room. In spite of his sudden infatuation by the sexual thunderbolt with which his marrow, his brain and all his nerves were quivering, however, Pierrot made a ludicrous but reasonable remark regarding the resistance of his mistress—since that is what she was about to be: "Women are often like crayfish; they only retreat in order better to be eaten."

Certainly, he would gladly have stolen kisses from the woman's Eyes, which were still scintillating beneath the veil with unexpected ferocity or seductive softness. Through the cobweb mesh, they were shining like two diabolical Eyes, with pale green irises in which phosphorescent glimmers lit up and blazed to accompany phrases that vibrated cheerfully: Eyes in which the reflection seemed to remain of the fire that burned the accursed cities, Sodom, Gomorrah, Seboim and Adama, in a little of the dead water of the asphalt lakes.

In truth, of that unknown woman, Pierrot and his Conscience only saw the elegant silhouette, the undulating movements, the rare and precious gestures, and, above all—no longer letting anything else be seen, at certain moments—the extraordinary Eyes, caressant or malevolent, from which the mysterious gaze of the sphinx flowed.

They were penetrating and lustful, they excited desire and folly, they sang, with light, quivering appeals, they wept the sobs by which one is enraptured; they rejected one who implores immediately after the reckless welcome; they were curious, those Eyes, curious to see, to love, to enable enjoyment, to cause suffering, to invite death.

And they were ingenuous Eyes, too, in which the soul of a child laughed.

At the base of the veil, the red line of greedy lips shone, a mouth of delight, a flower of pleasure.

The supper was served. Without touching it, however, they had both moved from the table to the divan, where they were sitting, with the Conscience opposite. Now, in a corner, she seemed pensive and indifferent, when suddenly, as she stood up, Pierrot precipitated himself to retain the ankles of the tawny-haired beauty and kissed her minuscule feet.

Did she esteem lovers who are proud, or would she offer herself? He murmured to her: "I kiss your knees."

She replied: "*Excelsior*, my dear."

Getting up, he tipped her back over the cushions; but, straightening her upper body and getting a grip on herself—the hands abandoned, however, and the mouth promising—she whipped him with a humorous remark.

At her knees again, he brushed the unknown woman with creeping and feverish fingers, gripping the black silk stockings over the frail ankles, caressing the slender limbs, and then—as she stopped, with a flash of the Eyes, the foraging under the skirts—gadding about the terracotta thighs, crushing his mouth into the bosom of the dress, where he thrilled himself with the hidden magic of womanhood.

Lifting his head again, he perceived a troubling smile of the demoness of the seven temptations. As he clutched a rounded rump, ambiguous, indecisive hips of an adolescent girl or ephebe, as his hands mounted to her breasts and clenched upon them, she said:

"What are you going to give me?"

"Everything I have is yours."

For him, she was the illusion; for Pierrot, that woman united all perfections; the more mysterious she remained, the more unknown she remained, the more absolutely he loved her, Her, and nothing but her. Not to mention that Pierrot had retained in his soul, ingenuous in spite of everything, the curiosity of precious children and adolescents before the mystery of Woman; although Woman is naturally a divinity, an Idol, this one appeared to him to be the ideal, a poem of mind and flesh, in whom were assembled all enchantments, and in her Eyes, lowered toward his, he read, not daring to believe it yet, the invitation to the voyage; he saw, in an ecstasy, in her green-gold irises, the nebulosity of their innumerable kisses.

His heart fainting, his voice strangled, he said: "I desire you, I love you, I adore you."

The smile of a mocking and fleeing fauness turned up the corners of her red mouth. The Conscience had drawn nearer; she seemed to be speaking to Pierrot: "I am Sentiment, I can follow you. You are sensuality, almost vice, you are Sensation. Don't be afraid, I'm still here, holding your hand."

What was the unknown woman thinking? She murmured: "Everything that you have is mine. Are you giving me your strength, your intelligence, your brain, your heart?"

"Everything."

"And your Conscience? *Will you sacrifice her for me?*"

Pierrot started. It was necessary to chase his comrade away. No, that he could not do. Then, her voice cruel, she broke the embrace; and under the fringed eyelids, the green-gold irises were hallucinatory. He was unwilling.

"My brain, my heart, my strength, you shall receive all that. What is it that you want?"

She repeated: "I want to kill your Conscience."

Her body was supple and avid; her Eyes sounded the hesitant man; a promised and desired voluptuousness uplifted the bosom and parted the red lips—the unknown lips—over the dazzling nacre of the teeth; the minuscule and perverse mouth, which was waiting, trembled, quivering for mad kisses, in the oblivion of the profound divan; the mouth was strongly and sweetly scented, like a flower, like a red carnation, with its peppery odor.

The demoness seemed all nervousness, all youth, but her adolescent and vicious grace nevertheless had the attraction of being crumpled. He gripped her again, wanting to drink from her eyes the dead water of the accursed lakes, wanting to conquer, to seal, to kiss that ironic and irritating mouth.

"I want to kill your Conscience. Do you consent to that?"

He could no longer resist; he whispered: "Yes."

"You won't have any remorse?"

"You'll no longer recoil?"

Slowly, with amorous prayers, manual and labial litanies, he rose—abolishing all past women in that unknown woman, dreaming all others in her—to the mouth of the chimera, in an exaltation; he rose toward the red and avid lips, whose quiver summoned him; he rose, his own lips quivering too, his eyes drunk on her, on her dear Eyes, taking the unpossessed in advance.

She fell back, coquettish and calculating; Pierrot's lips were over her lips, without touching them, aspiring the breath, the savor; now the Eyes, under the magnetism of the man, became troubled, vague, suddenly the color of absinthe.

A nearby sob put an end to the vertigo. In a corner of the room, the Conscience was weeping.

The unknown woman stood up, having picked up the lamp and placed it at her feet, on the carpet of the private room, in order to get undressed in the half-light; Pierrot remained kneeling, because she undressed slowly.

She doubtless knew her friend Pierrot well, the Conscience; ceasing to weep, she watched now, with an impish pout, knowing that possession often kills desire.

The unknown woman undressed.

First she took off her veil. Under the lace were others.

She unfastened her dress, but underneath another dress appeared, exactly similar. She took off her gloves, which hid others; then, sitting down, she crossed one leg over the other and kicked off little black satin shoes, on each of which were crossed, by way of buckles or adornments, two small bones, doubtless two phalanges from the fingers of a child's hand. She allowed the sight, up to the knee, of one of her slender legs, braced and harmonious in the silk stocking. And the beauty took off her stockings, which uncovered new ones absolutely similar.

The mysterious woman undressed incessantly, but she always remained clad in the same fashion, although she became increasingly thin. The Eyes had fascinating phosphorescent gleams, and she always maintained her exquisite contours—but the plurality of the contours became increasingly singular.

Pierrot wondered whether his dream was about to become ungraspable, like any infinite happiness.

Finally, she took off the last bloomers of lace and surah, took off the last black silk stockings, the last little shoes that had crossed microscopic bones, took off and dropped the final black gloves and a chemise that opened, from top to bottom, over her loveliness.

When she was completely, totally naked—her breasts were dreamlike, her arms dreamlike, awe were her legs, her thighs, and the brown moss, upon which his face wanted to descend, vanquished by pleasure, voluptuously saturated by the perfume of that flower of womanhood so desired, nostalgically, it seemed, forever; her legs and hips were immaterial, her breasts were dreamlike, her arms dreamlike—when she was completely naked.

There was no longer anything there.

✳

And outside, the death-throes of the masked ball, the sounds of the fête, gusts of extenuated quadrilles and the final waltzes, rhythms in shreds through the tulle of the night, supreme groans of violins, and into the cabinet, fatigued laughter, in the cabinet, the little abode of joy of the crimson divan, with the mirror striped with inscriptions, entered, sliding under the door, as into their coffin a few hours before, the white, the black, the crotchets, the quavers, the semiquavers, the demisemiquavers, sonorous and languorous wisps of a nearby piano—do, re, mi, fa— mi, mi, do, do—mi, mi, mi, mi—a languorous obsessively repetitive waltz. Tomorrow, again the pink roses, the white roses, the red roses, the gay lilacs, the hidden violets, will embalm April; spring will blow warm, intoxicating breezes; other fauns will run, sing and summon.

A waltz murmured—mi, mi, do, do, mi, mi—in the little abode of joy, so melancholy now, its languorous refrains.

Then, gently, the Conscience came toward Pierrot, who was sad, so sad, ready to weep, who dared not look up at her, whom he had pitilessly chased away in order to please that woman, who had so rapidly disappeared; and, a consoling sister, she said to him softly:

65

"Desire is worth more than anything else. What does the rest matter? You were not duped, *since you desired her enough to betray me.*"

XIV

Pierrot and his Conscience, heads bowed, remembering delightful nights of the time when they were young, telling themselves that since they emerged from the coffin they had seen many women, but none who had any amour other than that of gold, or even silver, resumed on foot the road to Montmartre cemetery.

Many collisions today, but almost no sparks struck. Pierrot had been ruined by his mistresses, but at least they had been foolish, with him, who was a fool, and neither lover had bought at three per cent.

The times are serious.

At dawn, the radiance of which was brightening the innumerable chimneys of Paris over the rooftops, both of them, fatigued by the night, went back into their vault.

And while they lay down again beneath their mortuary shroud, the Conscience said to Pierrot:

"Joy is very lugubrious. We only found one woman who realized the dream, and, like any ideal, we were not able to embrace her. We would have done better, companion, not to want the impossible, and, being counted among the dead, should have *stayed at home.*"

The Emerald Princess

A Tale of the Thousand and Second,
Third, Fourth and Fifth Nights

THE FIRST NIGHT
THE MORTAL KISS

I
The Nuptial Gong

BONG!

BONG!

Since dawn, like a shroud worn by nocturnal hands, the deafening plaint of the gong had enveloped the entire city.

BONG!

Its bronze maw spat out its powerful and heavy sounds. They transpierced the feverish expectation of all the individuals crowded together, who had quit their beds as soon as the appeal resounded.

BONG!

                  BONG!

Ten naked slaves with muscles as hard as cables, were scarcely sufficient to lift the enormous hammer that bought from the brazen moon, gigantic in its bronze armature, the grim summons whose symbolic echo struck the very hearts of the crowd. For, on the majority of faces, the folly of great hopes or that of great fears twisted the smiles.

BONG!

Was not the gong a kind of imposing clock, which would, among so many hours, sound one that was to be, for some handsome young men, radiant or mortal?

                  BONG!

That is why, while the slaves sweated around the infernal machine, the sordid crowd, breathless and swarming, huddled together, crushing one another, dominated by the savage rumor of the colossal hammer, which, falling back rhythmically, oppressed the city with its morose grandeur, as implacable as destiny.

BONG!

                  BONG!

II
The Low City

But was it what is conventionally called a city? Backed up against the flank of a crag, like pygmies at the feet of a colossus, it was more like a forest of hovels and huts: rudimentary habitations constructed with planks, with roofs of dry leaves and interlaced lianas, each one like a fragile nest linked to others by narrow, tortuous streets and strange bridges thrown hither and yon like rainbows. The water of streams, shiny and warmed by the sun, slid over the flanks of the giant crag like iridescent girdles over the ardent loins of a lover.

The inhabitants of those hovels exhaled poverty. The men lived half-naked. The women, on the contrary, dressed themselves in fabrics of bewildering colors. The majority dragged children behind them, clad in variously sized loincloths. All the reeks of slavery emanated from that place. The sole luxury of the inhabitants, the men in particular, consisted of rather singular designs which they spent hours painting, or having painted, on their torsos, or rather on their breasts,

From that swarming and sordid nightmare, that lugubrious mass, an emerald temple emerged, imposing and redoubtable, as everything is that is perfectly beautiful.

Above the low city, and the surrounding sites, that marvelous and fantastic citadel was radiant. On seeing it, one understood why the wretches assembled there continued to live in their mire, solely to be able to contemplate, in the evening, after the brutalization of work, until they went to sleep, the jewel that sprang forth in the night like a green star.

And the story that is about to be transcribed here, such as it was told by a djinni or a peri, on a night as beautiful as a dream, to a fisherman of stars of the twentieth century, happened in a country he knew not where or when . . . perhaps, in the very heart of the New World, where that powerful magician Gold can extract from the earth or the clouds an American movie that is an Oriental tale. Perhaps, too, in the land of California, on the set of a studio, in the brain of the narrator, a lamp more magical than Aladdin's has projected this sequence of black images, as living as light.[1]

The romance of Myram and Djila, the Emerald Princess, unfurls in the enchantment of the Orient, in the kingdom of the imagination, doubtless hundreds upon hundreds of years ago, in the time of the eloquent nights of Scheherazade and the sultan Haroun-al-Raschid.

But what does it matter?

When a story is told, the best thing is to abandon oneself fully to its caprice, as a handsome lover and his beloved abandon themselves to the enchantment of their ardor.

For, outside time, locale and space, isolated from the present, the past and the future, all stories of amour are fragments of eternity.

---

1 This curious reference might be an indication that part of the initial inspiration of the present story was supplied by the lavish 1924 silent movie *The Thief of Bagdad*, starring Douglas Fairbanks and directed by Raoul Walsh.

III
The Human Swell

BONG!

For hour after hour, hidden behind the walls of the sacred temple at the summit of the crag, the gong poured out its song: a song of love, certainly; a song of death, perhaps . . .

It covered with its resounding monotony the cries of the people of the low city, who, deserting their huts, were accumulating incessantly in the streets and the squares.

Almost all of them brought coarse fabrics with them, animal hides and flowery branches, and covered the rough ground with them. Then, on to those improvised carpets, their feverish hands threw flowers of all forms, all sizes and all colors. The ensemble formed the most picturesque of contrasts with the sad and dirty backcloth of the abandoned huts—for no one any longer remained in the hovels but impotent old men and a few young adolescents lingering before a copper plate in order to heighten their beauty. The moment, for them, was grave. Was it not a matter, for each of them, thanks to the aromatic oils adding luster to their hair, the necklaces emphasizing the strength or grace of their neck, and the arabesques expertly painted on their bodies, of standing out from all the rest?

BONG!

An increasing fever drew increasingly shrill cries from those women, men and children heaped up and bowed down for hours solely by the power of the gong, the hypnotic appeal of which held them there, anxious and tormented, avid to know the outcome of the festival that was upsetting their exceedingly simple souls and intoxicating their excessively feeble flesh.

The longer the gong resonated, the denser those crowds of people became, like cells juxtaposing themselves with one another, forming a single mass, a giant worm bordering the route that the imperial cortège would follow, a living block whose abrupt and puerile overflows, as ready for revolt as for adoration, and equally unworthy of either election.

BONG!

Within the clamor and formidable suggestion of the gong, the erotic power was sensible of the unknown and the mysterious, which extract the frissons of their interior being from the tenebrous humiliated individuals, in whom the quotidian routine of labor kills, puts to sleep or stifles the great instinctive currents that, alone, might raise them up.

BONG!

The appeal of the sumptuous and bizarre festival that the deafening rumble of the gong brought to those degenerate wretches, in order to extract them from the despotism of labor, spread over them a vertigo that made them howl with hope.

IV
The Nuptial Gong

BONG!

BONG!

BONG!

Finally, the song of the gong fell silent.

The low city knew now the imminent arrival of the Triple Splendor, queen and goddess, who lived in the Emerald Temple: Princess Djila, the Emerald Princess, the Heart-of-Rose Princess with the translucent eyes.

The sacred daughter of the old Emperor Satavahama,[1] she was to choose as she passed those who seemed to her to be the most handsome and the most vigorous of the young males of the city. Those designated by her desire had to leave everything in order to follow her, and win the honor of sharing the bed of the august heiress to a hundred kings and emperors, henceforth promoted to the rank of "Princes of the Blood." Parchments with the seals of the Princess would be sent to the families in order that a little of the high dignity conferred on their child or relative should fall back on them.

After the ceremony of the prenuptial procession, while

---

1 Satavahama is an alternative spelling, employed in both French and English texts, of Satavahana, an Indian dynasty based in the Deccan, which ruled that part of the subcontinent from the 271 B.C. to 30 B.C.

the gigantic gong resounded once again, the golden gates of the emerald palace would close forever on the elect.

And that is why, on that morning in spring, the crowd, like a monstrous spider ready to devour some paltry insect, stirred without knowing its own strength, along the path of the Exceedingly Powerful and Exceedingly Radiant Sovereign.

V

Myram, the Pearl Fisher

On the shores of the Black Lake bordering an exterior part of the low city to the northern side, stood a hut of humble aspect, but bright and charming. There, an ephebe answering to the name of Myram lived with his younger brother, Dao. If only by virtue of his beauty and his grace, one would have been struck by the sight of him, as before those predestined for an exceptional future.

In a face with an olive tint, his dark blue eyes, streaked with flecks of gold like summer nights, were fascinating, so moving and passionate was the gaze that filtered beneath the black fringe of long, curved lashes—how the houris would have envied them!

Myram fished in the deep waters for the jewel dedicated to Venus, the precious item "born of the wind, the atmosphere and celestial light," as it was named when invoked by young Brahmins after initiation, when a consecrated pearl is suspended around their neck in order to protect them from all harm.[1]

---

1 The motif of the two brothers and Myram's métier are reminiscent of George Bizet's opera *Les Pêcheurs de perles* (1863; tr. as *The Pearl Fish-*

During the warmest months of the year, until the equinox—or even later if the winds remained favorable, Myram was one of the most skilful fishers of pearl-bearing oysters. With his nostrils pinched by a bone clip and his fingers sheathed in leather to protect them from cuts, with his basket at his waist and attached to a stone, he descended at the end of a cable whose other end was held by other fishes aboard a moored boat.

More robust than many, he sometimes succeeded in remaining in the submarine enchantment for four or five minutes—but what risks there were! What frightful dangers there were, even though he wore around his neck a holy amulet to protect him against death, against the frightful and diabolical fish that lie in wait on the seabed and catch humans, the magnificent prey.

In the other seasons, Myram withdrew to his hut and enclosed himself alone with his future jewels. There was much discussion in the low city of the fashion in which Myram must work his pearls, for no other fisher offered, on market days, pearls of such a delicate gleam, as pure and as translucent. Some claimed to have seen around his hut the corpses of doves, which Myram had surely killed in order to make use of them, making them swallow the pearls in order to embellish them. Others affirmed that it was by means of other magical practices, more secret, that the fisher Myram succeeded in possessing the most dazzling marvels of the sea.

In reality, Myram had the science and the art of working pearls. With a fine blade in one hand and a smooth skin

---

ers), with a libretto by Eugène Cornon and Michel Carré, which is set in legendary times in Ceylon. Although the plots are entirely different, the similarity of background suggests that the opera might have been one of the principal influences on Champsaur's story.

in the other, he simply dedicated himself to long and admirable labor, which consisted of freeing each jewel, with patient delicacy, of the layers formed by various impurities that hid it from view. But of what skill he had to give proof! It required so little to remove from the Splendid all of its value, or diminish it irredeemably.

Thus Myram spent his days, attached to his labor, akin to an ardent, voluptuous poetry. And while embellishing his pearls, he also pursued a dream; for, just as the jewel destined to exalt feminine beauty forms slowly in the submarine flora, so, in the heart of the poor and magnificent Myram, the incomparable treasure of amour had crystallized.

On the day when, as she traversed the low city, Princess Djila had appeared to Myram for the first time, a hitherto unknown disturbance had taken possession of his soul. As a revolving sun illuminates the least and most arid corners, Amour, in a flash, had transformed him. He had understood the value of life, of light, and his heart had appeared to him to take flights from his breast, in an enraptured cry, toward a divinity, the Emerald Princess, a woman summarizing all women, a synthesis of the beauty of earth and heaven.

He had understood why, when he came back from fishing, his body exhausted by effort but stiffened by the hope of success, the gazes of the young women that he met became heavier and lingered upon him. He had understood their smiles, as soft as charms, and the perfumed attraction of their floating hair.

That day, in his turn, he had known the shock of desire that rises and descends, and descends again and rises again in the body, during certain instants as long as hours, as beautiful as dreams: the shock of the desire that then leaves the entire being bewildered and overturned.

That day, he had known the moving fascination of a face, all of whose contours form and reform incessantly, wherever one poses the eyes, and which envelops you like a spell, rendering distant and indifferent anything that is not it.

From then on he had decided, surpassing all possible measure of labor, to acquire enough splendid pearls to adorn himself richly in order that the one who had given life to such ardor would choose him as Prince of the Blood; and all his efforts were concentrated on the resolution to see that hope realized.

But alas, three times the nuptial gong had shaken the city, announcing the coming of the Princess. Three times, hieratic and troubling in her golden palanquin, she had designated the elect of her choice, and three times, Myram had felt himself brutally gripped by dolor.

And yet, cold despair had not succeeded in chilling his heart, for he had noticed, during her two last visits to the low city, that the soft and pensive eyes of his Idol had met the fervor of his gaze; and the last time, the tapering hand of the Emerald Pincess had been raised, sketching a gesture in his direction.

Why had she completed it toward another? Myram did not understand, even though he turned over a hundred thousand reasons in his head.

Immense love comports immense hope. Courageously, Myram returned to his arduous task. He was seen diving, determined to extract from submarine retreats the jewels worthy one day to adorn his beloved, for he could not imagine that a desire like his own could remain futile and uncomprehended. He toiled for hours over an auroral fragment, as if over his own heart, occupied in disengaging little by little from the nacreous sheath, the drool of brine or sand, the troubling mystery of the radiant tear of a violated oyster.

VI
The Interrogation

Today, when the anxious city is celebrating, Myram too has quit his work. The plate of polished metal, very shiny, interrogated as to his beauty, having given him an extraordinary confidence, he ornaments his ankles and his wrists, in an impetuous surge of hope, with jade bracelets. On his ocher flesh he designs gracious images. Like Persian princes, he attaches the symbolic pearl to his right ear. Is he not ennobled by the love he bears for the most Radiant of the radiant, the full Moon of his heart?

And, having finished dressing, he summons his young brother in order to ask him to attach to his neck the pearl necklaces that he wishes to give to Djila.

Although he is to accompany Myram in the city, Dao is not ornamented, for, knowing that Myram loves the Princess, he does not covet her, and does not seek to please her. Gratefully, Myram smiles at him.

Outside, the echo of the gong welcomes his flowering youth and strikes his desire. In passing, he darts a glance at the Black Lake and rests his weary eyes on the dark water, which always sends back to him the face that obsesses him, the cherished image.

"O lake," he murmurs, "tell me whether my amour

will be accomplished this time. Tell me whether Djila, my Princess . . ."

But before he has finished, and instead of the fortunate presage that a more ardent ray of the sun or the long-nursed, adored vision would have been, Myram, trembling with dread at the malefic sign, sees a frivolous little frog break the black lacquer of the water with its green response.

VII
Naradeva, the Sacred Guard

After the omnipotent appeal of the gong has ceased, there is a brief silence. The crowd, pressing more tightly, rises like a river in flood toward the mysterious crag, uttering clamors of satisfaction.

Up above, the heavy golden gate of the Palace has just rotated on its hinges, giving passage to the sacred guard of the Queen and Goddess Djila, the Emerald Princess, the Heart-of-Rose Princess.

On the threshold, the redoubtable stature of the giant Naradeva looms up. The shivering crowd salutes him with multiple howls, which seem from a distance to be a single growl, rumbling from breast to breast all along that road strewn with fabrics, hides, flowers and branches, over which the cortège will shortly pass.

The naked torso of Naradeva is bronzed, like all flesh touched since the cradle by the ardor of the sun. A thick green-gold tissue, split diagonally and sustained at the waist by a broad girdle of snakeskin, envelops him. His feet are shod in furs in which enormous raw emeralds sparkle.

Bracelets of gold and rubies around his arms and legs make their fires dance, and his ears seem elongated beneath the weight of heavy sapphires linked to one another by thin gold chains.

His enormous neck is bare, as is his cranium, tufted at the summit by a clump of white hair.

Naradeva comes down the steps covered in silks. His footfalls crush the ledges. His right arm traces grand gestures and his formidable hand, clenched on an ivory handle, lashes the air with a whip with golden thongs. The crowd makes itself more compact and retreats, its members protecting themselves instinctively, for each of the golden threads is terminated by a large diamond carved into a point, from the heart of which the sun brings forth a thousand scintillations.

"Make way for the Emerald Princess! Make way!" he proclaims, with his broad mouth.

The agitated diamonds collide with one another, and their whistling farandole traces bloody streaks in passing over the excessively close faces of curious children. The involuntary cry of a mother is stifled and suppressed, while taut arms seize the imprudent little ones. And Naradeva continues his route without the cowardly, subservient, tamed members of the crowd daring to utter a complaint.

"Make way for the Goddess! Make way for the Princess with the Heart-of-Rose! Make way!"

The gaze of the giant scans that multitude menacingly. Males and females, and children, draw closer and closer together as he passes, in order to avoid the diamantine golden lightning that causes blood to spurt from the flesh it touches.

In the eyes of that wretched mass, Naradeva is like a redoubtable God. An occult power inhabits his unique eye. The other eye is a phosphorescent emerald. Undoubtedly, that one was torn out by the gryphons in a terrible battle with his ancestors, the fabulous Arimaspes; they too had a single gaze, but situated in the middle of the torso.

"Make way for the Emerald Princess! Make way, vermin!"

The voice thunders without respite, to the turbulent rhythm of the thongs ripping the air.

Then, the women and children draw aside and prostrate themselves, for the uncovered palanquin has just surged forth from the threshold of the Emerald Palace, from which the incomparable Princess lets the limpid and ardent lightning of her gaze fall upon that multicolored route, where only the young adolescents, semi-naked and covered with adornments like young gods, are standing upright in the sunlight.

VIII
The Emerald Princess

Twelve young boys, their bodies coated with a metallic oil, precede the cortège. Only their loins are covered with scarlet silk. A turban of the same color coifs their heads; and, incrusted in the middle of their breasts, the sacred emblem shines: the green eye of emerald.

In a regular cadence, they advance, blowing into long curved ivory horns, the tips of which are directed toward the sky. The high-pitched sounds traverse the air, a fluid and fragile accompaniment to the glorious hymn that the bronze gong has taken up, with less violence.

And the variegated, prostrate crowd, howls its joy and its curiosity.

"Eaah! Eaah! Eaah!"

Following the young musicians are forty slaves, their bodies entirely painted green, linked to one another by a massive golden chain. They march slowly, the chain beating their loins and legs at every pace, sustaining the heavy, sculpted palanquin of the Most Precious.

"Make way for the Princess! Make way for the Divinity! Make way!" howls Naradeva, whose tall advancing stature dominates the plebeians in the whirling reflection of the golden thongs.

A Gem among gems, a Flower among flowers, a Rose among roses, lying on green brocade, the One finally appears who is the Inconceivable, the Most High and Most Attaching, the Infinitely Attractive Princess.

A turban clings to her temples, raised up very high in order to permit the sight of the sacred emerald that seems encrusted in the very center of her forehead, in the diaphanous flesh. It is a turban of white silk sewn with diamonds and gilded in the slightest of its pleats. To either side, attached by clasps of pearls, the sacred veil falls, supple and fine, over her shoulders, ornamented by thirteen necklaces, each of which is dazzling. Four are made of somber emeralds, three of pear-shaped pearls, five others are composed of diamonds intercalated with sapphires. Finally, the thirteenth, strange and luxurious, is a serpent whose scales are ornamented with gems of every species: topazes, amethysts, rubies, aquamarines and a quantity of jewels with barbaric names that only the coffers of a Princess of legend could contain. That reptile circling her neck like a caress is a talisman.

"Eaah! Eaah! Eaah!"

"Make way for the Goddess! Make way!"

Under the fluid lightness of her veils, also sparkling with precious stones, Djila allows herself to be divined entirely nude, ideal flesh, the perfection of the caress, the possibility of ecstasy and harmony, the personification of Beauty, the eternal fruit of the radiant secret that enriches nature and bears dream to its summit.

But no one can see the face of the Princess, whose mystery is covered by a veil with exceedingly fine mesh.

Only the miracle of her eyes is uncovered! They are two jewels of an unparalleled purity, in which all the mysterious and troubling reflections of Oriental magic play; two jewels under the protection of velvety eyelids as heavy as voluptuous promises trebling in their formulation. With such eyes, how can the face not be imagined as a vision of the paradise of Indra?

"Eaah! Eaah!"

"Make way for the Emerald Princess! Make way! Make way!"

BONG!

BONG!

IX
The Torches of Amour

In the deafening and monotonous noise, the gaze of magical irises dominates the whole of that breathless crowd like the luminous silence of moonlight above a demented nocturnal swell.

Precious and plaintive, contemplating all those young males, Djila allows herself to be numbed by the perfume of stupors rising toward her from the young adolescents, as spring sap rises in vigorous trees, under the first flashes of the solar rush.

"Djila! Djila! Queen of our nocturnal agitations!"

"Djila! Queen so divinely woman! Woman so delightfully Queen!"

From the troubling frisson that runs through the bodies of the ephebes intoxicated by hope, to the divine verses rising from cassolettes toward Lakshmi, which all the desires of men send forth on beholding her, the incense of praise is exhaled.

"Djila! May the flame of your possession illuminate my life as your beauty stiffens my lingam!"

"Djila! May your radiant hand designate me in passing, for I hold out toward you the torch of amour!"

Above quivering appeals, Djila is an ardent silence, but also ready to choose among so many radiations extended toward her with all the force of cupidity or passion.

"Eaah!"

"Make way, vermin! Make way!"

BONG!

The torsos of the forty slaves are gradually lustered by sweat. Over the slow and willful undulation of their green bodies, the palanquin of the Princess follows the route frayed by the redoubtable Naradeva.

And the crowd makes way respectfully, as the cortège passes by, which Djila dominates in the scintillation and irradiation of her beauty, so dazzling that it seems that there is no longer anything but the sun and Her.

X
The Choice of Princes

At a movement of the proud little hand and a sign from the precious fingers, the cortège stops. Naradeva advances alone. He has seen Desire shining in the eyes of the Princess . . . nothing but desire.

He approaches the person on whom the emerald light of her gaze has settled. He is a superb ephebe with flaxen hair and irises of a melancholy transparency.

"Your name, fortunate mortal?"

The young man's face is covered by an ardent pallor. In a voice invaded by emotion and pride, he articulates, turning toward the Most Beautiful: "Virahami, O goddess, to serve your Splendor."

And his head inclines to touch the ground in a symbolic gesture, while Naradeva proclaims:

"Approach, Virahami. Let me cover your shoulders with the mantle that consecrates you Prince of the Blood, and receive for your parents this present, the prize of your young virility."

Over the shoulders of Virahami, transfigured by joy, Naradeva hangs the heavy silver fabric maintained by a clasp in the form of a bird. To one of the members of the family he hands a bag of gold. Finally, prostrating himself before the new Prince, he slips on to his finger a ring ornamented with a sacred emerald and invites him to take his place in the cortège in front of the golden palanquin.

"Eaah! Eaah! Eaah!"

In the acclamations of the crowd, the howls of envy and stupor are perceptible of all the young males whose anxious visages are appealing to them the gaze of the taciturn sovereign.

And the cortège moves off, resuming its monotonous oscillation, preceded by Naradeva, who proclaims incessantly:

"Make way for the Goddess! Make way!"

Having arrived in the center of the low city, in a square, the final stage, the cortège stops. Grandiose is the spectacle of that effervescent crowd, above all, springing forth therefrom as its most beautiful pledges of adoration, that of the massed young males, offering their clusters inflated by flavorsome promises around the golden palanquin.

Toward Her, the radiant target of the arrows of the most devouring desires, all the diversity of smiles is directed: the smiles of debauchery, of cupidity, of dreamers, of the amorous, the ambitious and the innocent.

Among them, the pensive Djila searches for the most perfect.

Her long eyelids flutter several times, closing momentarily to protect fascinated pupils.

Myram is there.

His eyes are fixed upon her, delighting her with the humble imploration of their gaze, just as, by night, on the terraces, she contemplates the most beautiful stars in the heavens, and attains them by means of her desire.

She no longer knows whether it is the smile or the gaze of that amour that carries her beyond those quivering bodies offered to her caprice toward the excessive purity of a dream that defies everything. The mirror clutched by the sudden frisson of her hands, which is radiant in the sunlight, could not wound the eyes touched by its reflection more than the smile or gaze of that amour.

Emotionally, contemplating Myram's virginal adornments, she thinks about the superhuman labor, so perilous, that he must have accomplished in order to extract those pearls from the ocean waves. But she suppresses her admiration for the pearls and the fisher.

Beside Myram, resembling him, much as the aurora resembles a fire follet, stands his brother Dao, careless, it seems, of attracting the choice of the Princess. On the contrary, he only looks at her after having looked at his brother, as if, having understood, he is uniting them. Apart from a slight moustache for Dao, and the flame that illuminates Myram, the two brothers resemble one another closely enough to be confused.

What should she do? Choose the one that she loves, and whom her kiss will kill?

Djila senses that the crowd is waiting

Why do her fingers, surcharged with rings, not have the right to knot themselves around fingers that, in the depths of the dangerous sea, fish the pearl-bearing oysters?

Why, because of love, must she renounce love?

Meanwhile, a hymn of imploration rises toward her.

"Emerald Princess, deign . . ."

Now, at that moment of anguish, a rain of roses descends, and covers her golden palanquin. Here she is, the Rose among the roses. But the thoughtful crowd has removed from the marvelous flowers the thorns that might have wounded her hands. *Who will have the power to remove the mortal thorn from her, Princess Djila?*

And her terrible secret stifles her momentarily. A shadow stripes her brow, like the brutal flight of a black bird over a sunlit road.

Djila makes a sign to Naradeva. The sacred guard approaches, and before the two new elect, and then before their relatives, reiterates the same ceremony as for Varahami.

But one of the two is Dao, and the other is not Myram.

Then the cortège departs again, carrying the Princess, who, behind the double protection of the fan of plumes and her veil, reconstructs the smile destroyed by having not, out of love, accomplished the gesture that would have seized the unique love.

BONG!

And soon, Myram, torn apart, can no longer see anything of Her but the moonstones dangling from her ears, which are trembling like tears.

XI
Why His Brother Instead of Him?

No one any longer remains in the streets except for a few groups lingering to discuss the choice of the Princess, but Myram is still there. Bitterly, he is contemplating the roses strewing the ground, which, like him, have interested the cruel sovereign momentarily. And Myram wonders why, having fixed him with a gaze so tender—at least, it seemed so to him—it was Dao, his brother, whom her royal hand had designated?

What was the point of the hours spent sounding the sea to discover jewels worthy of her gaze? What was the point of the admirable black pearl that he kept jealously for her, hidden in his house, which no eye had soiled? What was the point of his heart swollen by devotion, his fervent hands, ready for all sacrifices for her Joy and her virginal body?

What was the point . . . ?

He thought abruptly about the dark Lake, and the temptation to hurl himself into it offered itself to him as a beneficent repose. But the memory of a gaze, so soft, that responded to his smile interposed itself, dissuading him from dying.

One last time, he gazed at the bruised roses, in the square that was now as empty as his hope.

He picked one up.

Who could tell whether, during its fall, that rose might have touched the Princess?

Then he resumed the route to his house, also solitary now.

And while walking, so weary and exhausted was he, that it seemed to him that the hammer of the nuptial gong was striking great blows upon his heart.

XII
Forsaken by Amour

BONG!
                    BONG!

BONG!

"Make way for the Goddess! Make way!
    "Eaah! Eaah!"

The howling crowd, trampling the roses that fervent hands continued to throw, is still following the cortège that is climbing toward the Emerald Palace. A further gesture from Djila has designated, silently and mechanically, a fourth ephebe; and while his relatives and friends express their frenetic joy in dancing, the sacred giant places the mantle upon him.

Now the cortège is climbing the monumental stairway hollowed out in the flank of the ruddy rock. The heavy gate opens like the golden maw of a magical dragon, and swallows, first the young Princes, before whom Naradeva prostrates himself as they pass by, and then the Princess, whose eyes, charged with a dolorous renunciation, turn involuntarily toward the city.

The whistle of the ivory horns ceases immediately. And, at the same time as the sumptuous portal closes behind the dispersed cortège, at the same time as, in the night, the dazzle of the daylight disappears, in the house from which Dao is absent, the sobbing of a poor pearl-fisher breaks the silence, while in the streets and alleyways, the crowd, from which four of its children have just been abstracted, that limited, stupid, howling crowd, returns to its misery with the satisfaction of a well-fed beast.

BONG!

BONG!

BONG!

XIII
The Four Elect

In the monumental courtyard, the slaves, with slow gestures, relieve their shoulders of the weight of the massive palanquin. Then, two by two, under the unique eye of Naradeva, they disappear through a trapdoor that has just lowered slowly. The rattle of their chains follows them into the darkness into which they plunge, like the sad echo of a plaint. Behind them, moved by invisible hands, the trapdoor rises up again and closes over the oblivion of their life.

Nothing is any longer visible then on the white flagstones, decorated with a single flower, but a flock of bluebirds whose wings, in passing, brush the new Princes, radiant, save for one, whose gaze is heavy with regret.

From another, smaller trapdoor, four adolescent girls emerge, like fays, their ankles circled with iron. They advance toward the Princess and, bowing down, kiss her bare feet. Getting up again, at a sign from the giant, they help Djila to quit the golden palanquin and place silken slippers on her feet. Then, the queen of enchantments takes the little slave-girls before the ephebes. The slaves bow profoundly, and while the Princess draws away, still mute, the slaves make a sign to the Princes to follow them.

At the extremity of a gallery in onyx and silver mosaic, is a round room. From there, four corridors depart; each one leads to an apartment reserved for the Princes. There, the group breaks up, and each ephebe follows his own slave-girl.

The apartments are strange and luxurious, with walls covered in brocade, their ebony floors with incrustations of nacre, and each one bears a name to which a legend is attached: there is the chamber of the dragon, that of the firebird, that of the cobra and that of the leopard. On the wall, near the bed, a painting is hung depicting the beast to which the room is consecrated.

Each of the Princes finds in his chamber the ornaments that he must put on in order to present himself before Djila. With languid gestures full of deferential admiration for their beauty, the slave-girls proceed with the dressing of the young men; they rub their flesh with unguents perfumed with musk and amber, which give it an aromatic velvet texture. An embalmed oil is spread over their hair, which enhances its shine. Loincloths woven of metal with a thousand gleams are knotted around their hips. Numerous bracelets are fastened around the wrists of the new stallions of the harem.

No turban will ornament the heads of the Princes until the nocturnal festival at which, in a special ceremony, the Emerald Princess will swathe those predestined foreheads herself. To the silver turbans a gem will be added that the Divinity will have chosen, the name of which the Prince will bear thereafter, in order that nothing shall any longer subsist of a wretched past.

Having finished, the skillful hands of the slaves offer the Princes a disk of reflective bronze; the young males contemplate themselves therein.

Dao, however, retains within himself the memory of the profound despair that had filled his brother's gaze when Djila, mysteriously cruel, had turned away in order to choose him, Dao, the only one of the quartet not to smile at her splendid and ornamented youth.

XIV
The Sacred Costume

While the young slave girls proceed with the adornment of the Elect, the Emerald Princess reposes in an octagonal room with walls encrusted with carved crystals, in which the most unexpected colors of light play curiously. Her eyes follow the limpid water in which, in a basin like an immense blooming corolla, fish with crimson scales pursue one another like thoughts. Minuscule monkeys gambol around, coming to cling to the tunic of their mistress, seemingly disputing, with fearful and impertinent gestures, the honor of tearing it. One of them having succeeded, Djila, amused to find herself thus undressed, gets up, and, heading toward the basin, allows the damaged fabric to slide away completely. The little monkeys chase one another, leaping.

Voluptuously, Djila plunges into the blue basin and frolics there, and then, making a sign to her slaves, escapes from the water, stretching herself.

From seven copper perfume-burners in the form of urns, mauve and rose swirls rise capriciously from pellets of sandalwood, jasmine and incense. Djila approaches. Her body, streaming with water, swivels slowly, rotates gently, arches harmoniously, swerving and undulating in the odorous spirals in order to impregnate itself with their perfume. And while she dances thus in a plaintive daze, the numbing vapors, drinking the humidity of her flesh as the sun aspires dew from calices in the morning, penetrate her and inebriate her.

Soon, without thinking any longer, she allows herself to be carried away, and then enveloped by the seven consecrated veils, which the lover must unfasten amorously, one by one. Around her ankles, expert hands seal golden serpents, and her neck, as long and fragile as the stem of an aquatic flower, is ornamented by a necklace formed, in accordance with custom, by seven rows of emeralds mounted on golden mesh.

On her forehead, a black turban divides above the sacred emerald that decorates her diaphanous brow. The astrologers and Magi attribute the emerald to the goddess Lakshmi, the sovereign of beauty and pleasure; could the divine amulet be better placed than on the forehead of the radiant Princess?

When the toilette is concluded, Naradeva appears. A silken loincloth circles his body. His unique eye shining with admiration at the sight of the Most Perfect, the sacred guard prostrates himself, announcing that the anxious Princes, gathered in the hall of honor, are awaiting the summons of amour.

A smile of pride parts Djila's lips. Her slaves wrap her in a long mantle spangled with diamonds.

Then, preceded by the grim guardian of her person, Djila goes out, followed by the malicious scintillation of the gaze of a little monkey.

XV
The Emperor Shatavahama and the Magus Brahms

In the shadow of crimson roses and somber foliage rose an ancient marble kiosk whose dilapidated walls were clad in a thick layer of moss. Floods of imperial sunlight penetrated through the door, which stood ajar.

In the unique circular room, on the carpet covering the ground, two strange old men are squatting, heads close together. An anxious crease wrinkles their foreheads more profoundly than the fissures traced on their visages by time. Poring over a partly unrolled parchment, they appear to be deeply absorbed by a number of entangled symbols, seemingly very irritated at not being able to decipher their meaning.

One of the two men is skeletally thin. His body is semi-clad in a black fabric dustier than the overgrown beard that disfigures him. He would be ugly and almost repulsive if eyes of a magical phosphorescence were not scintillating prodigiously in his visage: an intense, profound gaze, sounding regions beyond human vision; a gaze of surprising acuity capable of reading, one divines by its glare and blaze, everything within creatures that is hidden; a redoubtable and fascinating gaze, like that of birds whose nocturnal eyes penetrate without effort the secrets of the densest darkness. That individual is named Brahms, and that name is supplemented by the title of Magus.

The other old man, coiffed with a ridiculous turban, wears an assortment of three robes of unequal length, stacked one atop another, covered by an ample greenish-yellow mantle of atrocious tastelessness. His knotty fingers are charged with enormous rings. Around his neck four very beautiful necklaces are displayed, contrasting all the more with his grotesque accoutrement and the inelegance of his person. He is the Emperor Shatavahama, the father of the incomparable Djila.

The two fabulous old men, of almost legendary appearance, were inseparable friends. The majority of their time was spent thus, curbed together over ancient grimoires in search of a secret that the Magus and astrologer Brahms knew to be buried in the bosom of the subterranean depths of the Emerald Temple, the discovery of which concerned the happiness of the most Beautiful and most Radiant of all the princesses in the world.

The blue gleams of night falling over the crimson roses found them still there, elbow to elbow, in an almost religious meditation. But when, three times, the bronze appeal of the gong rang out, the Emperor, murmuring a few violent imprecations, got up, and went over the threshold with a hesitant tread.

Doubtless plunged in occult research, the Magus did not even raise his eyelids.

XVI
The Monarch's Observatory

As soon as he had emerged from their quotidian meditation, the Emperor headed for the hall of honor, but, suddenly changing his mind and modifying his route, he plunged beneath a low vault, only apparent after he had activated a mechanism hidden behind plants. There, after having climbed more than a hundred steps, painfully, he emerged into a rotunda that could barely have contained three people.

He ducked under a fur that he had placed there himself and waited for his eyes to become accustomed to the gloom of the redoubt—for on one side, the nacreous walls, finely divided by arabesques, permitted him to observe what was happening in the hall of honor.

At first, the light radiating from the torches down below blinded him, but his experienced eye gradually succeeded in discovering the shadows of unfamiliar individuals. Soon, he was able clearly to distinguish four handsome young ephebes—*doubtless*, he thought, *the new Princes of the Blood*—surrounding his daughter Djila.

With that, an enigmatic and cruel smile caused the sly and disquieting face of the Emperor Shatavahama to become even uglier.

XVII
The Magus and the Rose

Left alone, the magus Brahms started sighing at length, while his desiccated eyelids quivered over tearful eyes. Getting up in his turn, he traced large, incomprehensible designs on the bare wall with the tip of his wand, and the figures of monstrous animals, and finally, a firebird, a leopard, a dragon and a cobra. He was drawing, it seemed, prey to a strange delirium, which, holding him upright, with his long, supple stature stiffened, obliged him to carry out jerky gestures like those of an automaton. Even the tears that lustered his pallor with livid patches, appeared to be flowing without his being able to react.

Finally, he appeared to emerge from that alarming state, and, at the sight of the animals that he himself had drawn, he uttered a heart-rending cry. With his face to the ground he invoked the gods, repeating the name of the Princess several times over.

Then, after having rolled up he parchment and erased the signs on the wall, he enveloped himself in a shawl, whose gold had been tarnished by time, and went out, carefully closing the door, with the tread of an old man burdened by worries.

As he traversed the garden in order to go to the hall of honor, to which Djila had invited him, he stopped to pick a rose. Cautiously, his trembling fingers removed the thorns one by one. Only one remained, which he was about to detach like the others when the rose abruptly shed its petals.

The melancholy eyes of the Magus contemplated the devastated flower and the unique thorn.

He muttered an incantation and, throwing away the stem of the victorious dart, drew away, a little more bowed down, sadly shaking his head as if to signify his impotence.

XVIII
The Nuptial Feast

The banqueting hall of the palace, built as a terrace, over-looks the gardens and the green crag. Three sides decorated by a nacreous colonnade perforated like lace and a fourth formed by a colonnade of black marble ornamented with emeralds, frame the terrace of silver flagstones.

In the center there is a kind of nacre platform on which is set a massive golden table surrounded by low seats covered with feline pelts. On the table, all the accessories of the feast have their exterior faces garnished with precious stones.

In a corner of the terrace, the Princes, accompanied by their slave girls, are talking to one another in low voices, while the moonlight decorates their faces with bright arabesques.

Finally, here comes Djila.

Preceded by forty slaves bearing torches, the Princess, enveloped by that coppery flamboyance, resembles a maleficent apparition.

When she has taken the place of honor at the table, Naradeva presents her with a large black cushion on which four silver turbans are set, each decorated with a different gem.

Designated by his sovereign, the first ephebe chosen in the low city kneels down, and the august hands of the Princess circle his forehead, shining with passion, with the turban that is ornamented with a ruby cut in the form of a carbuncle. The ephebe, who becomes henceforth, by virtue of the Princess's choice, the Ruby Prince, bows profoundly.

And Dao, Myram's brother, approaching in his turn, receives the turban ornamented with the gem consecrated to the firmament, the precious stone that has the property of rendering virtuous, and of which it is said: "Whoever wears the sapphire will never be afraid."

The other two elect receive in their turn, with the same ceremony, the turbans in which the turquoise shines for one and the topaz for the other, two of the twelve sacred stones of the Celestial City.

The consecration concluded, Djila was indicating his place to each one when the Emperor Shatavahama arrived, out of breath from having quit his secret observatory too hastily. When he was seated, the Princes took their places.

And the feast commenced.

Dwarfs turbaned with picturesque silks—there was one that had a tiny one, even smaller than a dwarf—distribute the dishes with an almost magical skill and dexterity. In the meantime, the Princes' four slave girls, each having taken up a bizarre instrument, fill the air with languorous sonorities.

Now, while everyone savors the rarest fruits and drinks succulent liqueurs, snake-charmers, jugglers, naked dancers, little monkeys and white peacocks strive ingeniously to add merriment to the feast, in which, insidiously, a carnal fever takes possession of the guests, charmed by the perfumes, the music and the heady wines.

The drunken Emperor laughs uproariously.

Then Djila makes a sign to Naradeva and the sacred guard leaves, accompanied by the forty slaves and the dwarf servitors. No one any longer remains but the Emperor, the Princess, the four Elect and their slave girls, whose nervous hands are drawing acidic and lascivious sounds from the quivering strings. Then, behind a scarlet velvet door-curtain, the attentive and morose eyes of the Magus watch for the propitious moment.

The light of the torches trembles tragically in the nocturnal breeze, as light as a sigh, and the moment has come for Djila to decide which of the Princes will be her husband this evening.

She contemplates her provision of lovers, a trifle sad and feverish. Her eyes encounter heavy gazes and voluptuous appeals. Only the Sapphire Prince is motionless and distant. Djila remembers his grave voice when, soon after the sacred toilette, in the hall of honor, he said to her, staring at her imperiously:

"I am the brother of Myram, the most skillful of pearl-fishers."

He seemed to be begging thus to be released.

Above the banquet table, their eyes meet, complicitly, and she smiles at him, as at a brother. Then, in order not to yield to the atrocious temptation to seek Myram, the other, in him, and to struggle against the excessively clear invasion of a dream, Djila stands up and orders: "Prince Ruby . . . it is you that I shall keep this evening. Prince Sapphire. Prince Turquoise and Prince Topaz, you may retire."

Each of the Princes inclines in a genuflection before leaving, but only the Sapphire Prince, in a silence full of secret comprehension, dares to pose his lips respectfully on the bare foot of the mysterious Princess that his brother Myram adores . . . and whom, perhaps, She loves.

XIX
The Venomous Woman

The silver darts of the moonlight are breaking on the flag-stones, immediately devoured by the ardent flamboyance of torches.

The slave girls, singing now, are still plucking the melodious strings, save for one whose eyelids are closed as if to escape some bewitchment. Not far away, in fact, the Magus, who entered silently as soon as the dwarfs and the forty slaves departed, is staring at the young musiciennes with eyes charged with narcotizing effluvia. And although the light fingers continue to pour out harmony, their faces are gradually covered by a smooth pallor, and the dull pupils remain fixed, as if deprived of life, or full of a life over which a light veil has been extended, attenuating its brightness.

The Emperor Shatavahama is still drinking and laughing heavily every time, in trying to stand up, he staggers and has to hang on to the table.

The sacred guard, Naradeva, after having made sure that no indiscreet eye is spying on the Divinity, stands motionless against the vast black curtain that hides the door whose heavy bolts he has drawn.

The Ruby Prince, having drawn Djila to the low divan, envelops her with a wild passion of gestures, to which she responds gently, as if she were living a dream. And it is a dream, in fact, that she embraces, for beyond the face that, leaning over, burns her hands with kisses, the languid eyes of the Princess sees the handsome face of the fisher in whose right ear a pearl is stirring.

"Myram . . . ! Myram . . . !"

She whispers that name with a softness so fervent and so tender that the Ruby Prince raises his head joyfully, having heard nothing but the sigh—which he interprets as the confession of a desire.

Snatched from the dream by a frenetic prelude of expert caresses, Djila allows herself to be borne away by the reality. The veils are unfastened, and she appears, delivering to the dazzled eyes of the Ruby Prince the perfection of her beauty. Almost savagely, the young Prince takes possession of her.

But . . . at the precise instant precious among all instants, when the body and victorious amour bring their glorious offering, Djila's kiss, powerful and tenacious, unites the amorous junction of their lips with death. Djila's tongue darts ferociously into the avid mouth of the poor male in perdition.

The frenetic laughter of the drunken Emperor traverses the terrace at the same time as, further away, the Magus, extending his arms toward the heavens, moans a prayer. Distant and tensed, the young musiciennes are still playing, even so; and an atrocious smile passes over Naradeva's lips.

Pale, as if inert, Djila has closed her eyes, and in the silence of her absolute abandonment, she prolongs her kiss.

Suddenly, the enraptured young lover straightens up, surprised by the sharp pain of a sting, to which, in his enjoyment, he paid no heed, while an acid taste mingled with blood fills his mouth. He looks at Djila, interrogatively, while, bewildered by horror, he perceives between the fingers with which she is protecting her sensual lips, a tongue moving, terminating in a menacing dart like those reptiles possess.

He understands . . .

Fear prevents any cry for help—which would doubtless be vain—emerging from his throat. He would also like to howl his disgust, but his head is reeling, and, standing up, he totters, shaken by spasms.

Djila has quit the divan, and she draws away while the Ruby Prince, dragging himself, turns imploring eyes toward her, which his terror, despair and impotence render pitiful.

The Emperor sniggers and raps on the table like a drunken madman. Naradeva resembles an inexorable god. The Magus is still lamenting, his forehead raised toward the sky.

A cry, however, escapes the bosom of the Prince: "Venomous Woman! Venomous Woman!"

For a moment, he reels; then he comes to fall down, heavily, near one of the young musiciennes, who get to their feet with a start, abandoning their instruments, and flee, terrified.

The Princess approaches the cadaver of her lover, mutely, still placing her crossed hands over her mouth. She sees the image of the beautiful pearl-fisher, Myram, and the atrocity of her destiny fills her with a profound bitterness.

Gently, she frees her victim's head from the vice of the silver turban, and her eyes fall mechanically upon the ruby that ornaments it. She perceives that it is streaked. A drop of venom, spurting in that mortal amorous battle, had been sufficient, once more, to accord destiny with the legend that dictates that "the wearer of an impure stone is vowed to the worst evils."

XX
In the Darkness, Two Eyes of a Gazelle

Abruptly tearing herself from the anguish instinctively surging forth, the Princess recoils and shouts: "Take that corpse away! Quickly, take away that cadaver!"

And she collapses, with a sob.

Naradeva, having summoned slaves, gives them a sign to take away the remains of the young ephebe. Afterwards, he approaches the fainted Princess and, with strange gestures of tenderness, envelops her in a fur and seizes her in his powerful arms. And the Moon, the only eye that still has life on that terrace, knows by those gestures the secret amour in the heart of a monster.

Having reached he crystal chamber, Naradeva sets her down delicately on her bed and instructs the slaves to have extreme care for their mistress, for, he says, she is ill and sad.

Afterwards, in the night, he returns to his solitude and his meditations.

Meanwhile, up above, on the terrace, the Emperor Shatavahama is sleeping heavily, plunged in drunkenness.

The Magus is kneeling, imploring the gods to lighten the pure face of the martyr to destiny. In the paling torch-light, his visage, fervently emotional, becomes almost handsome. Even the nocturnal birds, brushing the terrace with their heavy flight, cannot break the ecstasy of his prayer.

In the Palace, silence—a poignant silence—has fallen again behind death, like a black veil over an altar, after the consummation of a sacrifice.

The three Princes, ignorant of their comrade's fate, are sleeping happily, perhaps dreaming of the kiss of the Radiant who has selected them, and will doubtless soon deign to choose them for the supreme kiss.

Except that, leaning on the foot of his bed, contemplating Dao, the brother of Myram, with a melancholy but resolute tenderness, his little slave, Yailee, is watching over the sleeping Sapphire Prince with the eyes of a gazelle.

THE SECOND NIGHT
SAVED FROM THE KISS

I
The Caprice of the Princess

Since the evening mortal to the Ruby Prince, Djila had retired to her crystal chamber. There, in the retreat of her tormented heart, she lived, assailed in turn by remorse and impotence before her destiny and the impossible struggle of her young heart, ardently extended toward amour. She turned over hundreds and thousands of questions in her pretty head, struck by an implacable destiny encrusted on the utmost purity of her forehead. And when she went out, it was only at the times when the young princes went out walking, in order to observe them without their suspecting it.

As for the princes, it was granted to them to take advantage of the magnificence of the park, only accompanied by their slaves, who guided them in accord with their desire, at any hour of the day or night. Having not seen Djila again, they imagined her savoring voluptuousness in the passionate arms of the Ruby Prince.

Twelve times the sun and the moon had exchanged their reign in the mystery of the heavens, and the Emerald Princess had not yet made her will known to her cockerels. They were saddened by this, save for the Sapphire Prince, who believed he had read in the fervent silence of two languid eyes a measureless devotion that he dared not accept—or reject.

One day, at the hour when they were all accustomed to meet, the imposing silhouette of Naradeva, the sacred guard, appeared. Beneath the coppery foliage where the three future lovers were chatting, he halted, the messenger of an enigmatic order.

He told the handsome ephebes that a feast had been organized for that very evening, in honor of the choice that she was to make among them of a new husband. They were therefore asked to put on their decorative costumes.

Then, Naradeva, after having bowed to them profoundly, left the Turquoise Prince and the Topaz Prince astonished by the short reign of their comrade, the first elected, each of them anxious to know whether he could bring to bear an attack and a resistance sufficient to retain the exceedingly whimsical sovereign for longer.

Only the Sapphire Prince, as he returned to his apartment, nurtured another, indefinable, anxiety in his heart.

II
Yailee with the Eyes of a Gazelle

Allowing his radiant nudity to be swathed by the charming gestures of his slave, the Sapphire Prince remained pensive. The perfumed oil flowing over his body penetrated him immediately, thanks to Yailee's fingers, which spread it skillfully, in spite of certain frissons that seemed to run through her occasionally. Observing her covertly, the Prince perceived the adolescent's disturbance, and felt himself rubbed by her with increasingly precise caresses.

To begin with, he spoke in a low voice, as if in extreme weakness. Encouraged by that softness, Yailee put her tremulous soul into her eyes, and Dao read further appeals in her sparkling pupils, beneath the almond-shaped eyelids, drowned by a distress inexpert in concealing its force.

Carried away by a sudden vertigo, he leaned over, and, lifting up the slave in his arms, he drank the tears that were pearling in her eyes like dewdrops.

Yailee abandoned herself. Her entire body was in the powerful arms, a virginal offering to the god Kama, finally discovered, to the victorious spring against which one no longer wishes to struggle. In her, the gushing joy flowed fresh and sweet, as a clear spring drawn from the rock descends softly and timidly, still seeking its path through the stones.

Meanwhile, the seductive tenderness of Dao facilitated the initial abandonment; the Sapphire Prince, pausing on the lips, suddenly marked the sacred slave girl, Yailee, with the burning seal of the first kiss.

Naked, radiant and perfect under the luminosity of caresses, she had before amour the happy smile of a little girl in the great benefit of the sunlight; and in the murmur of a sob of joy, she offered her body with her hands extended.

III
Amour Awakes

BONG!

The sound, like a blow to the heart, tore them brutally from amour, and in Yailee's eyes, terror suddenly appeared.

"Prince Sapphire, O my Master, O my lover!"

"What are you saying, Yailee? I love you, and if you are in danger, I'm ready to defend you."

"It's you, my beloved, who are risking your life here. I can't explain to you the frightful secret that is brooding in this palace, but my blood runs cold merely at the memory of what it has been given to me to see . . .

"The kiss of the Emerald Princess is like the bite of the most venomous serpents; it kills almost instantaneously. You must not be present at the feast this evening. I'm afraid that your beauty will cause you to be chosen by the Princess, and that would mean a horrible death by her venom.

"Listen, I implore you; it's not jealousy that is leading me astray. My love alone is giving me the strength to risk a frightful death myself by warning you. Listen, listen! Before the cruel Naradeva comes to fetch you to immolate you to the caprice of an accursed Princess, wrap yourself in these animal skins. And when he asks for you, I shall say that you are ill, and asleep.

"First of all, get dressed and go to bed, in order that you're ready to follow me when I return. I know a place to which I want to take you before fleeing . . . and you'll see everything. Afterwards, I'll show you the means by which we'll escape. Then you can go to the people, so odiously deceived, and you can reveal what you've learned. Then, come back and look for me, for my life is henceforth bound to your heart, a slave of your slightest desires, and a passionate servant of your happiness . . ."

A kiss completed the troubling revelation. A supreme embrace brought them together in the anguish and terror of the danger that might break the unparalleled enchantment. Then Yailee disappeared, as swift and light as a fay.

Immediately, the Sapphire Prince, following his lover's advice, lay down among the animal skins, pale and plaintive, seemingly very ill.

He heard the minutes falling in grains of sand, impatient to see the return of the angel who has saved him without thinking of her own peril. His heart beating forcefully, anxious and tense, Dao remained as if strangled by the invincible presentiment of a drama in which a victim would perish. He was afraid, very afraid. He was trembling. The more minutes passed without him seeing the adorable servant, the more he felt overcome by the evil sensation.

And yet, when he closed his eyes, burnished by a happy fatigue, he saw himself before the gods and before humans, taking for his wife the frail young sacred slave with the eyes of a gazelle, who had delivered to him with so much confidence and enthusiasm the treasure of her intact spring.

IV
The Poisonous Woman

As soon as she arrived in the hall of honor, all the slaves having thrown themselves face down on the ground as she passed by, the Emerald Princess made a sign to the giant Naradeva and said: "Why is the Sapphire Prince not present?"

"The Prince is ill and has asked to stay in his room. But his thoughts, he said, are around your Beauty."

"Prince Turquoise, and you, Prince Topaz, come closer. This evening, you will both stay with me."

As the two Princes took heir places by her sides, the Emperor Shatavahama came in, followed by the sad and intense Magus.

The table was laden with gold and silver platters of rare fruits, and heavy amphorae of heady wines.

In accordance with custom, Naradeva guarded the entrance door while watching the feast. The Emperor drank even more than usual, and the young Princes with slight embarrassment.

The four young slave girls played languorous and teasing melodies on their baroque instruments, which tormented the nerves. In their midst, Yailee had difficulty keeping calm. Suddenly, interrupting the tune with a sharp discord, a string on her instrument snapped.

Crimson emotion rose to her cheeks. Getting up, with a childlike, imploring gesture, she held out her instrument to the Princess. Djila made her a sign that she could withdraw. Yailee went out, having great difficulty dissimulating the tremor in her legs, and the black door-curtain fell back behind her, under the fixed stare of Naradeva.

Yailee ran to the apartment of the Sapphire Prince. Leaning over his bed, she put all her delicate and docile soul into the gift of her lips. Then, with a finger over her lips, she gestured to him to follow her.

First they went along a high gallery whose green marble was heightened by precious stones. At the end, Yailee turned round to make sure that no one was spying on them. Her light finger was shivering as it was posed on a silver arabesque that rotated three times, uncovering a secret door. Yailee pushed the door violently, so much had terror gradually harassed her. A multitude of galleries were offered. Without hesitation, she chose one, showing it to the silent Sapphire Prince.

At the extremity of a passage they stopped; Yailee had seized the Prince's hand in her own icy grip. The obscurity was dense, the silence impressive. Yailee's finger groped for a sculpture in the form of a serpent and produced a narrow and low opening. Yailee went through it first, her forehead almost touching the ground, and the fissure closed behind them, as if by magic.

They were pressed together in the same shivering, at the back of a minuscule rotunda whose walls were perforated on one side. Light filtered through that lacework, multiplied. Yailee huddled very close to her beloved and indicated to him with her gaze where he ought to look.

At first, receiving the light full in his face, the Sapphire Prince was dazzled. Gold flecks danced around him. Gradually, his eyes adapted and he realized that he was in an observatory placed above the hall of honor where, on the first evening, he had received the turban of a fiancé.

Now he was able to make out the golden table.

To either side of the Emerald Princess were the Turquoise and Topaz Princes. But where was the Ruby Prince?

While he was wondering, Yailee seized his hand, and raised it to her lips with a feverish haste, as if to draw the strength to remain there until the end without crying out.

The Sapphire Prince was still gazing.

The slaves and the dwarfs left. Naradeva closed the tenebrous curtain behind them. The Magus bent over, murmuring prayers. The drunken Emperor fell down the five sacred steps and remained on the ground, bewildered. The three slave girls were still playing, but their visages were closed, like corollas deprived of sunlight.

The Turquoise Prince surrounded Djila with his arms, extended in desire. The Adorable One leaned over, leaning slowly, slowly, and having parted the network of gold that hid her mouth, she planted her kiss on the Prince's lips.

The Emperor watches and sniggers. Naradeva smiles in a singular fashion. The head of the Magus inclines even more deeply, and the Topaz Prince has turned his head away.

Suddenly, a strident cry traverses the hall and rises like a flame all the way to the nacreous rotunda. Having turned back, the Topaz Prince sees his friend totter. But the Incomparable One fixes upon him her atrociously wide eyes, as if innocent of what is happening. He races toward her, snatches away the gold mesh that has fallen back over her lips, and seizes her mouth avidly.

Then a new scream rends the air vertically.

Frozen with horror, the Sapphire Prince sees Turquoise and Topaz spin around several times, and then fall, in convulsions.

The poisonous woman, standing against the golden table, has picked up roses, and she throws them over her victims with brief gestures, while a hissing sound emerges from her mouth, along with the horrible tongue of a cobra.

And the Sapphire Prince understands. With a gesture that surpasses his will, he casts off the nervous hands of Yailee, who is clinging to him, imploring him to be silent, and, breaking the nacreous arabesques he howls, at the top of his voice, like a madman:

"Accursed! Venomous Woman! Slut!"

V

The Alarm

A profound silence followed the Prince's roar. All visages turned toward the place from which the cry had come, and remained struck by stupor before the nacre wall and the agitating fist.

Only Naradeva seemed to suspect the truth. Djila, white with rage, bounded, and her fist struck a gong. The Emperor, sobered up and furious, looked up at his observatory, profaned by a sacrilege.

Slaves arrived at a run.

Naradeva indicated to them the elevated rotunda where the Prince, mad with delirium, continued to howl: "Accursed! Venomous Woman! Slut!"—in the language of the country and the epoch, naturally.

Her eyes darkened by hatred and shame, Djila was still striking her gong hectically, in order to drown out the cries of the furious Prince.

Naradeva, followed by slaves, had run to capture the guilty party. The three young musiciennes had dropped their instruments and, mute and terrorized, were huddling around the Emerald Princess.

The slaves, in an anguished coming-and-going through the palace, were transmitting orders and guarding all the exits in order to make sure of the capture of the criminal. And suddenly, on the superior order of Djila, the gigantic sacred gong invaded space with its deafening appeal, which fell upon the low city and raised the alarm.

BONG!

BONG!

BONG!

BONG!

That racket awakens everyone. The crowds rush out into the streets, frightened by the thunder of that enormous voice of bronze in the night.

In front of the huts, people hold discussions, wondering what mystery—doubtless tragic—is awakening the palace, allowing the light of hectic torches to be seen at the windows.

BONG!

BONG!

BONG!

BONG!

VI
Fortune Favors the Bold

In the nacreous rotunda the Sapphire Prince, breathless, exhausted by the incessantly increasing emotion, finally falls silent, ceasing his vengeful clamor, and with a supreme effort, his arms remain extended in the direction of the venomous Princess. And over the ebony flagstones of the banqueting hall, his blood traces a line of translucent rubies.

Yailee, panic-stricken, tracked by increasingly imminent and certain danger, could no longer find the mechanism of the door. She and her lover remained imprisoned. The footfalls of approaching slaves could be heard, dominated by the voice of Naradeva. Suddenly, Yailee, at the limit of emotion, uttered a cry as flaccid as a last sigh, and fainted.

In the opening of the broken-down door, Naradeva was sniggering victoriously. The Sapphire Prince, surrounded by slaves, darted a last glance toward his unconscious beloved, wishing that her sleep might be definitive, knowing the tortures to which Yailee would not fail to be subjected by the Princess if ever she woke from that nightmare.

Then, attempting the final audacity, he launched himself into the void through the enormous fissure, hanging on to the nacre panels decorating the high walls of the hall of honor. Thus, from one panel to the next, he advanced before the eyes of the enraged but impotent gaze of Naradeva, and under the furious gaze of Djila, who sensed Myram's brother escaping her. She watched him, mad with wrath, full of reluctant admiration for such courage.

But why did it have to be him who was the hero of that adventure, him, who had discovered that atrocious secret? Dao, now, was escaping, carrying with him a burden of which he would want to rid himself as soon as possible. It was necessary that he could not run to the low city crying to everyone the shame of the Emerald Princess, the infamy of the venomous woman.

And the Princess's heart of rose sobbed at the thought that Myram would despise her, would no longer surround her with the sentiment that elevated her so high that sometimes she had thought it possible one day to live that splendor, amour. And with all her strength, she desired the death of the audacious individual who must only want to live, now, for vengeance.

At every moment the Sapphire Prince risked being crushed on the flagstones of the palace. Suspended in the air, hanging on to fragile projections, a slightly abrupt gesture would suffice to cast him into the void, to reach an exceedingly flat denouement.

He no longer had much further to go before arriving at the great bay overlooking the park, where he might finally be able to escape that tragic hell.

Standing on the terrace, Djila watched, ferociously, waiting for the moment when Dao, his nerves abandoning him, would arrive above the black gulf of the park and the sacred lake.

However, the Prince was still advancing, under the rumor of insults and threats. Slaves were throwing torches, some of which, on reaching him, burned him slightly. His arms, increasingly bloody, nevertheless continued clinging to the silver ornaments of the hall of honor. An almost supernatural strength surged through him, pouring an indescribable courage into his veins, dominated by the determination to live in order to save Yailee, the gentle and tender beloved he had been obliged to leave in the hands of torturers, if there was still time.

He arrived now at the exterior of the terrace. His eyes, heavy with horror, perceived the gulf of the royal garden. Steel crampons were ripping his hands and shoulders, but the determination to flee made him insensible to all wounds, and, bloody and exhausted, he kept going regardless. Aiding himself with the sharp spikes, he reached the part of the palace where the park seemed to descend in order to be engulfed in the sacred lake.

Down below, on the terrace, the feverish Djila was still hoping to see slaves surge forth, finally bringing her the rebel. Through the park, torches in hand, illuminating all the corners here and there, they were running in vain, shouting as they ran, after the ungraspable fugitive.

The Sapphire Prince arrived at an immense wall overhanging the black water of the lake. The iron spikes were tearing him more and more. It seemed that they were multiplying at the very moment when he had need of them, as he wanted to succeed in escaping, concentrating his effort. He felt himself weakening and becoming frightened.

Along the wall, snakes were now crawling through the thick moss, hidden in order to take him by surprise. Before then, the Prince, weakened and maddened, lost his head. Preferring a brutal death to that venomous embrace, like that of the Princess's kiss, he let himself fall into the glaucous lake, this time entrusting himself to hazard.

His thin and supple body turned in his fall through space, at the same time as a torch was hurled after him from above. And the water closed over the man and the torch, like a fan of black plumes.

Reanimated by the shock and the cold, protected by the moonless obscurity of the sky swarming with stars, he struggled against the tenebrous water with the despair of a reckless individual betting his last chip.

Rearing up on their tails at the top of the wall, a hundred serpents, their eyes fixed, without apparent life, watched that vertiginous escape.

He was swimming on the surface of the water with an imperceptible splashing. The greatest difficulty was steering. Fortunately, a voice, which he thought he recognized, shouted: "This way! This way! Courage!"

Myram, thanks to his piercing eyes, had perceived that form, which was surely trying to escape a danger, and he guided him thus. At intervals, the fugitive dived, for arrows launched from the Emerald Place flew above his head like streaks.

Dao, chilled by the black-tinted water, felt an arm grip him, and he allowed himself to be held, like a weary little child, without having consciousness enough to wonder whether the arms were those of a friend or an enemy.

"Brother! Let yourself be carried, Dao!"

The voice was soft and ardent, and it seemed to him, once again, that he had heard it before. It was so warm, too, that the unfortunate let himself go as he listened to it, without attempting to perceive the words that it was pronouncing.

VII
Thrown to the Serpents

In the hall of honor, Djila has taken her place on the divan which has been fatal to so many elected princes. She is wielding a large whip with steel thongs, over the bare backs of slaves who kneel down, one by one, ashamed of not having captured the precious Sapphire Prince.

The black door-curtain with silver embroideries is raised and Naradeva appears, bearing in his powerful extended arms the charming unconscious body of the slave girl Yailee.

"Here is the slut who betrayed you, Princess!"

And he presents the gracious body for chastisement.

The Princess almost smiles. The young musciennes allow a sob to escape. Then Djila lashes all three of them until the blood flows, with the whip with the metallic thongs, in order to teach them to be quiet.

"Naradeva, tell the slaves, quickly, to pick up the corpses of the two Princes and give them as fodder to the cobras."

When the cadavers have been taken away and have disappeared, the slaves return and line up, daggers extended. Naradeva has taken his place by the black curtain again. The Emperor is sitting down, satisfied.

Only the Magus is still praying, perpetually.

Beneath a blow of the whip delivered by the Princess, Yailee is reanimated. She blushes to see herself almost naked before so many scornful, hostile gazes, and her haggard eyes search for a cherished presence, the Sapphire Prince.

"He has fled!" proclaims the Princess, with a cruel satisfaction. "He has abandoned you!"

"Oh, my lover!" is all that Yailee murmurs, with the sweet joy of sacrifice that simple and faithful souls experience—because for her, it is important, above all, that he, the Sapphire Prince, be saved.

Her eyes encounter the unique gaze of Naradeva, and a cry of fright passes over her lips—for she has understood, now, what her torture will be. She murmurs: "My lover! My sweet lover!"

Naradeva's whip with the diamond-tipped extremities lashes her furiously, and the poor girl collapses, stifled by pain.

In a low voice, Naradeva gives orders. The slaves withdraw. Djila contemplates the slender body shaken by sobs.

Biting roses, she throws them over her, ironically. Then, turning to the three young musiciennes, under the threat of Naradeva's golden whip, she orders them to play. Immediately, heart-rending notes vibrate sadly.

The door-curtain is raised again. Carrying a glass cage in which reptiles are competing in suppleness, the slaves traverse the hall cautiously. The imprisoned reptiles are set down before Djila, who gazes at Yailee impassively. The trembling child has understood; she wrings her little hands.

Imploring the mercy of being allowed to live, Yailee is lifted up. A pitiless stroke of the whip replies to her. She moans, and her blood flows, drop by drop. To flee the redoubtable cage, she recoils, but feels her bare back pricked by the points of several spears. Devastated, she no longer knows which to choose. Her heart is like a gong beneath a hammer.

Two hands seize her, the two hands of a slave who is about to throw her alive to the serpents. In the desperate struggle, she frees herself. Her last narrow girdle having come undone, her last veil falls too. She springs forth, completely naked this time, so delicate, so frail and so beautiful, and above all so touching. She senses that some of the slaves desire her. She looks at them, standing up proudly, as if before death, and senses, by virtue of her heart and the love it bears, how much greater she is among them all, and how much above them all.

Tearing from her finger the emerald ring that marked her slavery, she throws it to the ground. Then she closes her eyes, finally avid for no matter what repose.

The slave girls, her companions, are playing, and it seems that their music is descending from the heavens to

121

calm her. She thinks about the gods and whether she is going to suffer there henceforth, and whether, on high, one day, her beloved will be returned to her.

Two more brutal hands grip her and master her. She can no longer see clearly, and does not know to whom those hands belong. They are surely not the hands of her prince, for those were gentle and caressant, and these are bruising her.

A beloved form, in the fog of her mind, is designed before her. And her tears flow, abundantly, baring appeasement to her poor childish heart.

"Prince Sapphire!" she sighs.

She can no longer see anything but him . . . fortunately, for the violent hands that have seized her now enclose her in the glass cage where the serpents are agitating in vehement torsions toward their prey.

All those mouths, with sharp darts, are open to compete for her.

The visage of the little sacred slave is calm, almost ecstatic, and the glances that Yailee darts around her are like happy smiles.

"Prince Sapphire! My lover!"

An entire jazz of serpents hissing over her head makes her lose all consciousness. They have chilled her with fear, winding around her frail nudity. That pell-mell of horrid darts, of shrill, discordant sounds, of mouths gaping to devour her is changed into caresses, which absorb her and intoxicate her.

The three slave girls accompany, with tender and plaintive chords, the death-throes devoid of revolt of the tender Yailee, whom love has enabled, in such a short time, to blossom and close again.

VIII
The Secret of the Emerald Palace

Myram had deposited his cherished burden on the gilded sand. People approached, and all of them, in the darkness, interrogated him. But Myram, certain that only a great suffering could have determined Dao to flee the Palace, imposing silence on the curious, carried his brother home.

The news of that unexpected return was already traversing the low city as a dagger cuts through a breast, and everyone felt touched in the heart. Were people not happy in the Emerald Palace, from which that young ephebe, chosen, had run away? For what reason? Had he preferred to risk death in order to return to his comrades, the people, his companions in misery? And men and women gathered, interrogating one another under the stars, awaiting the dawn, seeking to pierce the enigma. It was known already that the young man was Dao, the brother of Myram, the most skillful and most handsome of pearl fishers.

Myram had laid him down on his old bed in their cabin. Dao allowed himself to be cared for with a haggard gaze that seemed to be still inhabited by terror. He repeated, in a distant voice:

"Yailee . . . ! My little Yailee . . . !"

No one understood who the Prince was talking about.

Finally, he seemed to return to life, to reality. Myram, leaning over his bed, tried to help him to reconstruct his memory, which seemed somewhat demolished.

"Do you remember, Dao? I'm your brother, Myram, and you were chosen by Djila, the Princess that I love, that I adore, as you know . . ."

"The Accursed! The Venomous Woman! The Venomous Woman!" cried Dao, sitting up in bed, with horror.

Myram went pale. He launched at his brother a despairing glance, as if to beg him not to repeat such ugly words. But, driven in spite of himself by the desire to know, he begged, squeezing his clenched fists around his brother's wrists: "Explain your sacrilegious words!"

Then Dao gathered his strength. Tears sprang from his face, ravaged by the frightful moments he had been forced to live. And, in a bruised voice, he confided the terrible story to Myram and those of his friends who were there.

IX
Myram, Avenger of Martyrs

"Eaah! Eaah!"

That simplistic exclamation, the same for joy as for terror in those poor folk, multiplied in the huts, in the streets and the tangled alleyways, summarized, throughout the low city, the growling of the wretched. At Dao's story, repeated from mouth to mouth, the crowd became delirious, inflamed by wrath.

Tortured, Myram listened to the people. With great difficulty, in the midst of such baleful events, he rediscovered his amour.

So, the Princess he loved was that horrible and fatal woman. And the more Dao spoke, the more Myram felt an intense void penetrating his heart. He shivered, his teeth clenched over the words of dolorous hatred that he wanted to spring forth. For adoration had been succeeded by rancor, grim hatred against the adored individual culpable of so many odious sins.

In a tumultuous frisson, the story was still passing from mouth to mouth. Myram felt his passion being transformed into a terrible desire for punishment. All the devotion that lived in him for the one he had placed so high in his heart became bile and anger.

Outside, the story was already on the lips of mothers in mourning for the loss of their sons. Some wept, others howled, but the same cry was everywhere:

"Vengeance! Vengeance!"

And toward the Emerald Palace, up above on its crag, all fists, clenched in distress, were raised. Myram had the impression, coming from all those humble folk, that he had a duty to punish so many atrocities. Between his desires, his exalted amour, and the hatred that is still born of amour, Myram was like a bamboo stem swaying in a high wind. Around him, a thousand voices were crying: "Death to Djila! Death to the venomous woman!"

Finally, resolute, standing on a rock, he proclaimed:

"Listen! Let us not fight *en masse*, for the defenses of the Palace are far more redoubtable than your weapons. The golden gate will never open, even before your combined efforts, and that revolt would end in carnage. Have faith in me! Alone, before that ignoble creature, culpable of so many horrors, I shall avenge your sobs and your mourning. I shall depart, alone, and go to her, and may I die immediately if I, Myram, whom you all know, do not tear out her filthy tongue with these very hands and do not throw it to the dogs and the pigs to be devoured. Oh, the prostitute!

"You shall have her! We shall all have her!"

There was a clamor:

"Vive Myram!

"Glory to Myram!"

"Honor to Myram!"

"Eaah! Vive . . . ! Vive Myram!"

And the hero went on, in a resounding voice: "The sacrifice of my body is easy or me, now that my soul has been torn out. This very evening, by favor of darkness, I shall depart for the Palace. The gods will protect me and I shall succeed, I'm sure, in reaching it victoriously. And in that redoubtable enclosure, I shall take hold of the Emerald Princess; with this dagger I shall personally cut out her tongue with its deadly dart."

"Glory to the handsome Myram! Glory!"

The men raised frenetic hands toward him, the women blew him kisses from their extended fingers. He was offered weapons and vestments, but he did not accept any. His heart was filled by a world of dolor and hatred and he did not want to take anything but that heart *to Her*.

In the eyes of those humble folk, Myram was a savior, but in his own eyes he was no more than a poor individual torn apart by a woman and a dream.

To his woe alone was the sound of all those voices, of pitiful beings forever defeated by superior powers, sweet. The eternally oppressed murmured their gratitude to him. He did not know the names of those people; he did not want to know them—but he experienced an infinite tenderness for those who were suffering. He received their affection as a supreme donation, from which to draw the courage to go forth to fight the tyrant, the venomous woman, the woman he adored. And his torment drew tears from him, for them and for himself—and for Her, the most wretched of all.

After a summary repast, Myram left. On the narrow square, where the zigzag side streets terminated, the crowd gave him an ovation. Women knelt down as he passed by, praying to the gods of heaven to protect such bravery.

The mothers of the Ruby Prince, the Topaz Prince and the Turquoise Prince kissed his hands; he brushed their foreheads with his pure and dolorous lips.

"I shall avenge all of you!" he cried. "I swear it by Siva!"

Sobs rose from breathless bosoms. The admirable ephebe, Myram, the most scintillating of pearl fishers, standing in the radiance of the full moon, pale and grave, had the air of a holocaust offered to the Asiatic gods in expiation of the temporary revolt of the wretched—who dared, for a moment, to raise up their necks, tamed beneath the yoke, like those of domesticated buffaloes, under the weight of their destiny.

THE THIRD NIGHT
DISGUISES OF THE HEART

I
Two Unknown Suns

Myram marched, his heart heavy with the harsh verity with which hazard had just turned his life upside down. Before him were entangled execrable visions in which Djila was by turns an adored woman and a dangerous reptile. However, his stride strove to remain energetic and he advanced with the decision of those who, expecting some nightmare, are in haste to encounter it.

He arrived, in the mauve and gray veils of the dusk, at the foot of the somber crag dominated by the palace.

Myram stopped, stumbling.

Up above, the phosphorescence of two Eyes scrutinized the density of the increasing darkness. He had just enough time to dive into the brushwood in order to escape the indiscretion of those watchful eyes. Crouched in the shadows, waiting for the glimmers to move, the pearl fisher wondered what the strange animal was that was watching so grimly.

The gleams had shifted. Myram crawled through the clumps of plants and the moss that covered the stones, climbing to assault the fantastic crag. It seemed to take a long time, for the effort he was making against the torment of his thought and against the difficulties of his ascent oppressed him slowly.

On the highest terrace, the colossal silhouette of Naradeva loomed up. Beside him was the tiger-hippopotamus whose terrible Eyes turned their redoubtable gaze in all directions.

How could he succeed in getting past unperceived? Tentatively, he approached a gilded door that he had discovered, and searching its precious ornamentation, he tried to discover its secret.

He stifled a cry before the myriads of monstrous ants, voracious and pullutaing, that precipitated toward him. What could he do against that horde? Drawing from its sheath the dagger he was wearing at his waist, he was clearing his skin with precipitate scraping when, at the same moment, the enormous fiery pupils paused on the fronton of the door guarded by the giant ants.

Myram froze, terrified, murmuring a hectic invocation to the Trimurti of Brahma, Siva and Vishnu.

Finally, Naradeva closed his unique eye, and the horrible feline, the tiger with the maw of a hippopotamus and Eyes like beacons, was only turning toward the low city the danger of the two unknown suns of its gleaming gaze.

It seemed to Myram that a voice breathed in his ear, encouraging him to audacity:

"If you want to be a Prince, you must merit it."

II
The Talisman

In order to avoid the enormous and hostile ants, Myram has retreated, ducking down beneath the protection of a rock external to that first terrace. He perceives, in touching the rock, that the form of a serpent seems to be engraved thereon. He presses down with his hand upon that sign. To his great surprise, the stone trembles and is slowly displaced, allowing the perception of a black hole. Plunging his gaze into it, Myram sees fantastic green glimmers rising at intervals from the deep hollow. His eyes adapt to the glaucous atmosphere, and soon he distinguishes crude steps, seemingly scaly, reminiscent of a serpent's back.

Having slid into the secret stairway, he advances prudently and discovers, as he goes along, that the mysterious emerald gleams that struck him a little while ago originate from a liquid trickling in droplets along the walls of the narrow staircase. He places his palms on the wall. They are sticky, and it is difficult to pull his hands away again.

He continues his route, but gradually, he totters, the ground having started to move. Bending down, he palpates it. Then, in a start of repulsion and terror, he verifies that he is now walking over thousands of toads, and that it is their frightful drool that is covering the walls.

Making a violent effort, he hastens to continue, in order to escape as quickly as possible from the repulsive contact, but not wanting to retreat. The further he goes, however, the more the purulent mass increases. He sinks into it, gradually bogged down, and the nasty creatures spread the stinking mucus, the first touch of which had momentarily immobilized him with aversion, over his legs.

Suddenly, in a corner of the wall, a small sculpted serpent appears to him like a sign of salvation. Raising his hand to reach what he believes to be a talisman, he palpates it, his entire body stiffening in the effort to escape certain death in the glutinous embrace, increasingly repugnant to him, of that moving green-tinted filth.

As soon as he has pressed upon the emerald eye of the serpent, however, the toads disappear, as if by magic: an ephemeral horror. And the displaced slab offers Myram the new issue of a corridor into which he immediately sets forth.

Scarcely has he taken a few steps than the slab falls back into place behind him, blocking the opening. Thus absolutely isolated, Myram, his heart unyielding, is now moving with feverish haste along a corridor bathed with a light similar to the reflections of the emerald that sparkles in the forehead of Djila, the accursed beloved.

III
The Grotto of Temptations

A gracious oval, like a yoni, terminates the corridor that Myram travels rapidly. On passing his body through that opening he feels a light breeze caress his face.

Myram is in a marvelous grotto resembling a nacreous seashell. A spring freshness greets him like a smile. Mauve, pink and blue petals rain down, with a snow of down and pollen as light as a radiant awakening of nature. In the utmost depths of this paradise, a cascade sheds its pearly drops over the tender foliage of green, azure and roseate branches reminiscent of peacock's tails. And all of that April palpitates like fans or the wings of butterflies.

Suddenly, from that curious flora, extraordinary but recognizable nevertheless, another miracle springs forth, an unparalleled dazzle: an entirely feminine flora.

Dancing, laughing, singing, swirling like nacreous elves, naked adolescent girls pursue one another. Their gracious hands agitate, dispensing pleasure, scarves and kisses. Their eyes dart gazes, each of which, like a new spell, winds in a spiral around the surprised and charmed Myram.

From what heaven do these bodies agitated by amorous folly descend, those murmurous, flavorsome mouths, offerings to voluptuousness, those breasts as beautiful as the apples of the Garden of Houris, promising infinite and delirious tenderness, those legs whose supple magnetism summons the enlacements of brutal embraces and languorous raptures?

Some, lively, agile and laughing, are swimming, ascending, descending or transversally, in the white or pink fluids of the cascade, evoking for Myram the fascinating pearls that he so often extracted from dangerous waters.

Before that enchantment of spring and women, the troubling aromas of which a warm breeze causes to exhale more powerfully. Myram stops in the midst of those daughters of gardens and water. Such a bewitchment is emitted by those odorous beauties that he is perhaps about to allow himself to be caught by a siren whose open mouth is offered like a ripe, split pomegranate. He abandons himself to so many adorable visions—*almost as beautiful as Djila*, he thinks . . .

Almost! Poor Myram!

Because, for him, in spite of the reasons for hatred amassed by her crimes over the memory of Djila, he still finds her more perfect, worthy of being elected queen, infinitely superior to all the troubling creatures who are smiling at him.

Is he about to allow himself to be deflected from his goal, the punishment of the Venomous Woman? Will he be conquered forever by this seductive monster?

In the nick of time, he perceives a serpent crawling in the grass toward a rose-bush decked with pink roses. Returning to reality, Myram falls upon and seizes that living talisman, which has already saved him from the atrocious entanglement of the toads, and which will save him from the temptations that are assailing him at close range. He waves it like a victorious flag, clutching it preciously in the midst of the smiles and dances.

And now the cascade vanishes in a final deluge of whimsical reflections, and the mouths like butterflies, the arms like scarves, the breasts like sensual golden fruits, the callipygian visions, the split yonis as velvety as peaches, also scatter, disappearing in a quivering of multicolored gauzes and crystalline laughter.

IV
The Last Sirens

After the horrible dangers, the charming obstacles: he has triumphed over them all. Myram feels his body and face in several places in order to be quite certain that he has not been duped by the ambushes of a dream.

Preparing to continue his strange route, he looks around, seeking the direction in which to go. To his great amazement, he, who knows nothing but the huts of the low city, sees houses looming up before him, the highest stories of which seem to be puncturing and scraping the sky.

Where, in what unknown country, can these monumental buildings rise up, compared with which the Palace of the Emerald Princess appears minuscule? A gray sky weighs upon those audacious constructions, as if to avenge itself for being thus violated—all the more so as that leaden sky is also traversed, at an astounding speed, by gigantic metallic birds whose wings brush the terraces that terminate those houses, and bridges launched through the air.

Myriads of men and women are agitating in that incredible landscape, nightmarish for him, which changes its appearance at every instant. They are like a horde of barbarians rushing to assault an infernal city, bristling like a fortress. Howling and whistling can be heard. An entire world of creatures, wheeled palanquins as closed as the cages of wild beasts, can be seen. Tubes in the form of towers spit out black, malodorous clouds. And all those terrible noises seem to dominate the folly of an immense city ravaged by evil djinn and hurling toward an implacably sad sky the racket of a frantic life.

Myram now applies his trembling hands to his ears. He is in a realm of extraordinary inventions. Powerful wheels spin, enormous metal shafts move back and forth, gears grip other gears, and in that living forest of unknown mechanisms, appearing to him, through that phantasmagoria, with the face of Djila, the person who governs everything, the *Instigatress*, attracts him, the recompense of conquerors, Woman, with the smile that the great granite sphinx of the land of Egypt forms every dawn.

And the high buildings of twenty stories whose terraces scrape the sky reappear. Myram hurls himself onto one of those formidable edifices. Looking around in order to assure himself that no new danger menaces him, he observes that he is only in a room with bare white walls devoid of ornamentation. Sitting there, each at a table, three adolescent girls are raising and bringing down their fingers with a prodigious speed. They are clad in dresses so tight, like elegant sheaths, that Myram can distinguish their gracious forms perfectly. Their legs, visible up to the knees, are covered in a web of spidery silk the color of flesh; and, which astonishes even more, all three have short hair, entirely shaven over the nape. Having never seen such women, Myra evokes, involuntarily, emotionally, the long, perfumed hair of Djila, in which he dreams of falling asleep after amour, as one falls asleep when one is sheltered from noise in a profound forest.

At every regular movement, however, the slender fingers of the adolescents each strike a minuscule white disk bearing a black symbol. At times, a faint bell is heard, while on the strange instrument, which Myram has never seen in the hands of any musicienne of the low city or the Palace, a black roller advances, retreats, and then resumes its initial position under an adroit gesture of the hands of the girls, whose tapering fingers are performing such a pretty saraband over the white disks with the black symbols.

Myram's amazement is even greater on seeing a parchment emerge from the instrument covered in black characters, similar to those that ornament the little disks on which the agile fingers are tapping rhythmically. His eyes interrogate one of those gracious fays with the hairless napes. Then she begins to chirp volubly in a language that is melodious but which he does not understand. Seeing her lack of success, the young woman sits down again, pulling a face. Another stands up, stares at him ardently and, without saying a word, approaches him very closely and offers him her hand.

He is about to seize it, perhaps to kiss it, when he sees, to his good fortune, a flexible bright snake with ruby eyes wound around the wrist of the temptress like a bracelet. Then Myram remembers that the reptile in question saves

135

him from peril and, turning away from the temptress with the short hair, the shaven nape, the bare breasts and the demonic machines, he caresses his fetish gently, as if imploring mercy.[1]

And once again, along with the extraordinary city, the great iron birds and the baroque slender instruments, the three girls who were enticing the pearl fisher while tapping their writing machines vanished.

Then, in the mist of the pink and white powder that those original sirens—he had seen many others when he plunged into the oceanic depths in pursuit of pearls—were putting over their cheeks and the tips of their noses with a soft pad, there were three bursts of laughter.

And Myram, that peril avoided, found himself confronted by an interminable staircase, rising as if to the sky, all the way to the stars, with steps encrusted with diamonds, sapphires and turquoises, at the foot of which he let himself fall, exhausted by fatigue and suppressed emotion.

V
The Struggle with the Spider

As if momentarily brutalized by bewilderment, Myram remained in a numb torpor for a brief while. Having

---

1 If an autobiographical interlude in *Tuer les vieux! Jouir!* (1925; tr. as "Kill the Old! Enjoy!") can be trusted, in this phase of his career, the aged Champsaur dictated his works to amanuenses hired from local agencies by the hour, wherever he happened to be, some of whom were doubtless young, wore their hair in the bobs fashionable at the time, and might well have typed directly from his dictation rather than employing intermediary shorthand. From the viewpoint of the author, they might indeed have represented the last sirens.

raised his head, he saw that the summit of the steps was bathed by an opaline light. A grave resolution reset his features, and, with a new valor, he began the ascent of the magnificent stairway that seemed to extend all the way to the sun.

Very rapidly, his mind dispelling the fatigue as inopportune, Myram climbed the diamond-studded steps.

And he penetrated into a cavern whose walls were covered with velvety moss. In the center of that grotto was an immense web with silver threads, doubtless woven by a colossal and hidden spider. Behind it opened a path from which the blue-tinted glow, the glimmer of first light that had guided Myram, emerged, and which now dazzled him like a nascent sunrise.

Myram seized a dagger, determined to cut through the network that barred the passage. In spite of the thrusts however, under which the web shook, the mesh remained intact.

Suddenly, in front of him, covered in dirty hair, its green eyes darting opaline gleams that burned him, Myram saw an enormous spider appear. Like the preceding vision, its disproportionate abdomen and its head with eyes like lanterns surpassed all human imagination.

Adroitly, the gigantic spider was suspended in the intersection of the threads, menacingly, at the center of its web. Myram felt a chill of fear. Around him, everything seemed vertiginous and tormented. He was about to flee, but the shades of the murdered young lovers, poisoned by the venom of the Emerald Princess, barred his path.

He had to go on, all the way to the end.

Drawing his dagger again, he launched himself into a terrible, ferocious combat with the monster that was attempting to seize him. Three times, the audacious fisher succeeded in cutting off a leg; and finally, he was able to plunge his weapon into one of the eyes, each glance of which inflicted a burn.

Then, a horrible groan made the cavern tremble. From the hollow, empty orbit a sticky liquid escaped. The spider clung desperately to the strands of its web, while a spasm caused the brute to totter. And from that height, it fell, and crashed into the ground with a muffled thud.

Swiftly, Myram approached the dying monster, from the punctured eye of which a filthy and sticky mucus was flowing, and he noticed that as the dying eye was emptied out, the more swollen and shinier the other became. He moved closer. The punctured eye continued to leak a sticky fluid. Then, quickly, life seemed to abandon the entire hideous body—but the intact eye remained brilliant, disengaging increasingly ardent fire.

His garments torn, his body clawed, Myram, with a supreme gesture, tried to plunge his weapon into that mysterious glow, but the weapon slid away. The eye was no longer anything but a transparent ball of fire surrounded by a crystal. As for the spider, it had become a cadaver, collapsing by degrees, which was quickly reduced to an impalpable dust.

Soon, there was no longer anything on the ground but a strange, gross ball. Trembling, but determined to fathom the enigma, Myram seized it in his hands. At the same moment, a great crack was heard and Myram saw the web, which none of his thrusts had been able to sever, slowly fall away and crumble at his feet.

Now, poring over that luminous sphere, Myram turned it back and forth in his feverish hands, resolved to extract its flamboyant secret.

VI
The Magic Ball

Gripping it with an immeasurable hope, Myram did not budge, curbed over the crystal. It seemed to him that he could see strange living corpuscles inside it. Lending it a more sustained attention, he distinguished a form that gradually became more precise: that of an old man whose face was raised toward the sky, invoking the gods.

Myram quickly realized that the images in the crystal were merely a reflection arriving magically from elsewhere. He sought in vain to understand from where; in vain he turned the ball around and around; it was always the same form, a magus in meditation, that it reflected.

The cell in which the old man was praying was small and rather wretched. A smoky torch was blazing there. Suddenly, the attitude of the magus changed; it became that of an individual surprised by the arrival of someone else.

In fact, a woman came in.

And the anxious Myram recognized Princess Djila, the person whom he wanted with all his might to hate, and to hate recklessly. She was, as usual, veiled, but her admirable eyes were scintillating, charged with fear. Her febrile gestures denoted a dolorous disquiet.

Having not had time to reflect upon that unexpected apparition, Myram then saw an exquisite hall where Djila was preparing for her ablutions. As she shook herself, naked in the beneficent water, however, while the little monkeys smitten with the beauty of their mistress gamboled around the bathing pool, the white-haired old man reappeared. Myram, dazzled by the resplendent nudity of Djila, saw the old man—who was none other than the magus Brahms—prostrate himself and then stand up again, contemplating the entirely unclad Princess, in order to prostrate himself a further three times.

And, left alone, the Magus traced mysterious signs in mid-air, which seemed to be addressed to someone else, who could not be Djila, since she had disappeared from the ball, taking with her all the beauty of the world—and Myram understood then that the signs were addressed to him, the poor pearl fisher.

Filled with astonishment beyond measure, the pearl fisher wondered by what miracle the Magus was aware of, and, above all, was protecting, his coming. And, his mind immediately extended toward the One of whom his heart could no longer efface the naked image, Myram thought, and hoped, that Djila wanted him to be victorious.

A great strength filled his soul then. He felt ready to attempt anything and to smash any obstacles in order to reach the radiant Princess and to penetrate, finally, the enigma that surrounded her.

Why was she Venomous?

Raising his head, he perceived the light of dawn. He thought that he was approaching the palace of the Princess, whose beauty, surely, created that light; and, rising to his feet, with the magic ball in his hands, he set forth.

VII
The Ascent Toward the Sun and Destiny

A new courage invaded his heart. He penetrated into the long corridor from which the daylight came.

He had already been marching for some time and had not yet glimpsed its extremity. The light, however, was becoming brighter and the corridor more distinct. On the walls, very high in spite of the narrowness of the path, symbolic designs were engraved, and the slenderness of serpents often recurred as a decorative theme. Incrustations of emeralds, sacred stones, heightened their splendor, the sculptures also adorned with diamonds, magnificent sapphires and gilded topazes. As if in a waking dream, Myram passed by all these fortunes, all these preciosities, while a mysterious voice incited him perpetually to hurry.

In any case, the fever of reaching the goal, in spite of the worst dangers, made him shiver, and his heart was beating forcefully and unevenly. Cool effluvia reached him and now he was breathing beneficent air.

The corridor ended abruptly.

And he finally understood why he could not perceive the daylight. A narrow stairway rose up before him to a great height, allowing a glimpse, at the top, of a fragment of the sky.

He had, therefore, traversed all the secret grottoes of the sacred rock. Where would he be, then, when he arrived at the summit of the steep staircase?

Myram reflected that it was better to do battle in broad daylight than in these mysterious and diabolical lairs. He went up the stairs very rapidly, in haste to reach the goal; but at the summit, the apparition in flesh and bone of the fakir that he had first seen in the fantastic crystal ball stupefied him

The old man was standing on the final step, in daylight gilded by the sun. He looked at Myram and smiled at him; then he held out his arms to him. The crystal ball, into which the young warrior then gazed, no longer reflected anything but a vague translucent light.

Myram's eyes grew wide with surprise, and the venerable fakir, gently and silently, descended the steps that separated the two of them. He placed a thin yellow finger over his livid lips, and beckoned to the young man to follow him.

Having reached the supreme step again, he slid his fleshless hand over the arabesques, and in the glory of the rising sun, a golden panel opened.

VIII
The Fakir's Explanation

Old Brahms, turning round then, spoke to him in the low and sententious voice possessed by those from whom no earthly secret remains hidden for long, and who even know how to read human destinies in the celestial arcana. He confided to young Myram:

"By means of you, O handsome ephebe, the chosen instrument in the powerful hands of the gods, destiny will be accomplished. And I pray that Siva will recompense your magnificent bravery. Amour, I hope, will obtain the victory. But you come charged with hatred and vengeance, and your heart is mute, and your fist is armed with a dagger, sacred by virtue of the brown blood of the monster that you have battled. In your hands, Myram, you have a weapon even more terrible than your steel blade. You have the enchanted ball that permitted you to see me a little while ago. For you, it is the soul of the spider, which is devoted to you because, by killing it, you have delivered it from the cruel yoke of life.

"The spider was the transformation, operated by the gods of the emerald rock, of the Empress, the mother of Djila, who deceived her husband, the sacred Emperor, with one of the giant cobras of the golden temple. She gave birth to her daughter Djila, and the gods, to punish her, caused the Emerald Princess to be born with a tongue with venomous darts.

"The Emperor did not know what to think when Naradeva, the imperial guard, who had followed the unfaithful Empress one day into the temple where the cobras lived in peace, discovered the horrible rendezvous and denounced her treacherously. Immediately, the furious Emperor had the unworthy spouse put in chains, and had her thrown into the subterranean palace, a thousand years old, whose existence was unknown to everyone except the divine Emperor and me, his humble servant.

"I witnessed, Myram—yes, I witnessed—that frightful ceremony, and I was the last to remain with my august mistress in the unknown temple, near the staircase where you and I met.

"I was about to recommend my beloved Empress, for she was very gentle, to invoke the gods of the subterranean temple, when she began crying with all her might: 'Save my child! Save my child!' And as the gods remained silent, she blasphemed against them. Then, in the infernal racket, as if the entire secret temple was about to crumble, I saw that poor mother changed into a monstrous spider, a repugnant beast.

"I could do nothing except climb back up to the sunlight, frightened by that vision of horror, and, without saying anything to anyone, including the Emperor, I kept to myself the terrible secret that you have unveiled, young hero, and vanquished. Now, you only have one peril to risk, the worst of all, which is not imprinted with any mystery: the encounter with Naradeva, the sacred guard, who watches over the young goddess Djila day and night.

"As for me, the poor old fakir of the temple, I am returning to my parchments and my manuscripts, which permitted me to divine your approach and to see you. But you are still arriving too soon for me, for I have not been able to decipher the hieroglyphs of the gods that announce the destiny of the daughter of the serpent Metis, Djila, the Most High and the Most Beautiful, whom you cherish in the depths of your heart."

"No, fakir, I do not cherish her, for I want to kill with this dagger the Venomous Woman whose mortal kiss has made so many of my brothers fall forever into the eternal night. I hate her! I hate her! *I hate her!*"

"No, my son, you love her."

IX
Naradeva, the Sacred Guard

With those words, the Fakir drew away. Before disappearing, however, he turned to Myram and, with his ivory finger, he showed him the golden breach that he had caused to open by means of a magical pressure.

"Go that way, and follow the road without making a sound, for you will arrive directly in the great hall of honor in the palace, and Naradeva might perhaps be asleep there."

Having said that, he left Myram alone, whose soul was troubled by these unexpected revelations.

Emboldened by that venerable aid, he insinuated himself cautiously into the corridor, and raised a door-curtain embroidered with chimeras, which gave access to a small square room, one panel of which was gilded and admirably perforated. Through it, one could easily see an enormous nacreous hall.

How could he get into it?

The eyes of the indiscreet individual became accustomed to the solar light that gilded the great bay and the terrace, glimpsed from his refuge. Myram was able to discern in a few seconds the sacred sign that ought to open the perforated panel. The image of the little serpent, the talisman that he knew so well, was engraved almost at floor level. A slight pressure on the ornamental reptile caused the panel to slide quietly aside.

Myram took a step forward. He found himself in the immense hall. Instinctively, he hid, to begin with, under a golden table on which there was an extraordinary disorder. Quickly recovering his bravery, he inspected all the doors, but he saw nothing. Heading toward the heavy velvet door-curtain then, he lifted it up lightly, and did not perceive that old Brahms had hidden himself there and was following his audacious gestures attentively.

Recognizing then the plan that Dao[1] had indicated to him, Myram no longer hesitated. With the greatest prudence, however, pausing at the slightest sound, he headed toward the crystal chamber where Djila, the infamous poisonous woman, was—who, in spite of the unwitting

---

1 The original text has "Mao," but the invocation of that name in a context drawn from Hindu mythology, would be very odd; I have assumed that it is a misprint, and that the reference is to an indication of the layout of the palace given to Myram by his brother.

nature of her crimes, as the fakir had told him, nevertheless merited an implacable punishment.

In his emotion, his foot collided with a silver perfumeburner. At that sound, in front of a door magnificently sculpted with precious stones, which was closed, a magnificently muscled colossus rose to his feet, like a mighty living spring, upon the steps of iridescent glass, and looked in the direction of the intruder.

Quietly, heavily, Naradeva, the sacred guard of the Empress, took a few steps in the direction of the young madman. With a ferocious snigger, he saw Myram close by, daring to stand up to him. Then, he mounted to the highest step in front of his Goddess's door, and waited for the imprudent and sacrilegious individual, protecting the entrance with his two arms, parted to form a cross.

The combat was furious. Naradeva lashed out with his steel whip with diamond tips at each approach of the young fisher, who fell to the ground with dolorous plaints—but got up again immediately. Blood was trickling over his tumefied face, and his eyes were haggard, still troubled by a vision. His comrades, poisoned by the Venomous Woman, appeared to him again in that supreme combat.

Myram's dagger, meanwhile, deified by the blood of the spider, had already entered profoundly into the horrible coppery flesh of the sacred guard; but Naradeva appeared insensible, and responded to him with dolorous whiplashes that lacerated him atrociously.

All his brothers were before him, encouraging him, giving him a supernatural strength and energy. Like a furious madman, he struck Naradeva's flesh all over his body, and, clinging desperately to the giant's legs, finally achieving a small victory, he tripped him up.

Then Myram, in his combative dementia, thought of the crystal ball, which he had deposited on the floor, having more confidence in his steel weapon. In the blink of an eye he picked it up and threw it, like an enormous stone, into the face of the colossus, who was getting up, seething with rage, raising his two redoubtable arms.

With a thunderous noise, which the anxious crowd in the low city heard, the soul of the spider shattered. Behind the precious door, the Princess with the Heart of a Rose uttered a loud scream, and armed herself with a spear with five cutting edges, waiting for the hero she loved.

The heavy mass of the sacred guard collapsed and slid down the gilded steps.

Naradeva, his skull crushed, horribly pulverized, lay on the silver flagstones.

From the mysterious ball a viscous brown liquid flowed incessantly, inundating the inanimate body of Naradeva.

Discreet and muffled footfalls caused Myram to turn around, and he saw, at the extremity of the vast gallery, three slave girls, ocher-tinted dolls, who were gazing at the spectacle, terrified.

THE FOURTH NIGHT
AMOUR TRIUMPHANT

I
The Love Stronger than Death

With a violent push, Myram thrusts aside the enormous corpse of Naradeva, which is impeding his passage, and launches himself on to the stairway leading to the crystal chamber. In the fantastic golden decorations of the door that forbids the approach, Myram easily finds the design of the sacred serpent. He presses the ruby forming its head, and the door deploys like a fan.

Behind it, a gold grille erects a supreme defense. Through the perforations, Myram recognizes Djila, who, doubtless resolved to defend herself to the death, is holding a spear in her hand. Her resplendent face is naked; it is thus that he can see the horrible tongue, the cause of so many deaths.

The Princess, recognizing Myram, utters a great sigh and recoils, further and further, her wide eyes invaded by a great pain.

Myra searches with one hand, which is not trembling involuntarily, for the serpent design. The talisman immediately found again, the arabesques lift up, the grille separates into two, and each of its sides, which the hero supposes to be magical, disappears into the wall of silver and crystal.

The heart-rending and tragic moment is about to sound: it will bring punishment.

His garments torn away, his face soiled with blood, marked all over his body by wounds and the tracks of the whip with diamond-tipped thongs, Myram, almost naked, has stopped in the middle of the room, before the Princess. He seems to be hesitating.

His hand refuses to act . . .

? ! ? ! ? ! ? ! ?

Djila contemplates him and divines in him a heart that is constrained to hatred by a grim dolor.

"Myram . . . ! Myram . . . !"

In spite of her, that name had departed, as if sprung from the nucleus of a flame long enclosed by ashes.

So, Myram had come. He had braved everything, achieved victory everywhere, in spite of the multiple dangers of the route.

He had come.

He had come!

But alas, it was the thirst to avenge his brothers of the low city that had put so much courage and so much audacity into that body, the harmony of which was laid bare by the shredded clothing.

Myram observes Djila, and his gaze tries to decipher what the Princess—the woman he loves, and must kill—is thinking. Anger and admiration are in combat within him, coloring his face. And when Djila, pale, as if proffering herself, drops her spear, Myram feels his heart fill with an infinite pity; and the words of the Magus, inviting him to pardon unwitting sins, return to his memory.

At the same time, however, the vision of so many beautiful youths scythed down imposes itself upon him, and, stiffening himself, Myram advances toward her. He is trembling with an implacable resolution. Above Djila, his hand rises. The Princess does not recoil. With a meek resignation, she thinks about the radiant voluptuousness of dying by his hand, having only been able to live for him.

In order that he might contemplate her in her total splendor, she rejects with a light hand the precious veils that cover her, and, beneath the gleaming dagger in Myram's quivering hand, which seems impotent to strike, she allows the royalty of her perfection to appear in its carnal radiance. At the same time, she murmurs, like an ardent prayer, a passionate litany:

"O Myram, soul of my life and life of my soul, You who adore me and whom I adore, You who my hand has never chosen, in spite of the wound of my desire that is corroding my heart, because I did not want, even to satisfy an immense joy, to deliver you to oblivion . . . blessed be the gods, O Myram, that have put that weapon in your cherished hand. You will be delivering an unhappy woman from an impossible amour.

"Accomplish your mission, then, O my only, my unique amour! Djila will die without rancor, blessing you, and I shall carry away the great joy of finally having been touched by you.

"Beloved, hasten to redden your blade with my blood. Strike the heart of the woman who, glad to die by your hand, will not even have the magnificent consolation of a last kiss. Strike the place of my heart. Then, lean over me. For, in my last breath, I shall pronounce your name . . ."

Myram's arm falls back. The dagger drops from his hand. He surrounds Djila with his arms and carries her away, as the sole trophy worthy of his triumph.

In a sob that is so sweet a response, a consent of tenderness and gratitude, Djila abandons herself to the ardent embrace, her eyes closed, one hand over her lips, to drive away from her again the temptation of the mortal kiss.

Delicately, Myram places Djila on the cushions of all hues, which resemble enormous petals that must have been ripped from all kinds of fantastic flowers, in order to strew the nuptial couch where the beloved will know the first embrace, the incomparable imprints of which are never effaced from the flesh.

He kneels down. And Myram forgets everything that is not her, and everything that is not their amour, for he is certain that Djila loves him. The involuntary renunciation that led to her never choosing him when she went to the low city, and, at that very moment, the touching gesture of the most perfect hands in the world joined to protect him from her mouth, were convincing proofs of her love.

"Djila! Djila . . . ! Djila . . . !"

That exclamation, long contained by Myram, quivers and expands around the beloved, the venomous woman, like a beneficent rain. Tears run down the hero's face, soothing him and so many emotions supported. And here and there on the admirable body of the adored one, he sows kisses . . . kisses . . . and kisses . . .

He envelopes the one who was Inaccessible with caresses and passionate words:

"O Djila, I love you . . .

"Djila, I have always loved you . . .

"Djila, grant me the supreme kiss, the one that will break the horror of my destiny, in order that I might die by you, by your lips, as I would have wanted to live for them alone . . .

"Djila, my sovereign, let our senses swoon, in the intoxication of our confounded beings, and let the first kiss of amour that my lips have known be the one that kills . . .

"My life is yours! Djila, my beloved, you are an enchantment so prodigious and so great that it is sufficient for an entire life, for the beauty of the world."

With eyes lustrous with tears, Djila contemplated Myram. She drew him toward her with an aristocratic and resolute gesture. And while he continued to sing the intoxication of his heart and his magnificent joy, she mopped his bloody flesh with fine bright muslins and cradled his trembling heart with soft gazes.

Myram continued: "O Djila, your kiss! Djila, give me your kiss, to calm my suffering and rejoice my twenty years with an enchanting death."

Myram's lips run over her shoulders, over her neck, over her perfumed hair, still seeking to reach the fatal and chosen primal nest. But Djila resists, turning her head, refusing her maleficent mouth, always refusing—refusing to give death to that astounded lover.

And brutally, Myram takes hold of her wrists, tips back her face, and, as one tastes a fruit a long time awaited, an eternal happiness, presses himself against her, prevents the divinity from fleeing, takes possession of that primal lotus, henceforth devoid of revolt, and imprisons it . . .

✳

Awakened abruptly after a time that neither Myram nor Djila were able to measure, they contemplate one another with eyes magnified by visions of death.

152

"Make your voice heard again, my beloved, in order that, until my last breath, this evening, it will intoxicate me . . .

"Djila, your voice is like a pardon . . .

"It is a caress, a moonbeam in the dark . . ."

Bur Djila is oppressed by emotion. She is sobbing. The words remain in her throat. She can only contemplate him, and, with her hands wrapped round Myram's dagger, which she has just seized silently, she prepares to follow him into oblivion.

And, leaning toward one another, united in their identical destiny, Myram and Djila embrace one another recklessly. Death gazes upon those lovers, still indecisive, doubtless astonished to find them so generous and so beautiful—worthy in every respect of life.

II
The Venomous Woman Purified

Very quietly, in a panel of the crystal wall, arabesques have just shifted. Djila and Myram, enlaced, who are awaiting the effects of the mortal kiss, shiver nervously, and watch a hidden door open. The Goddess holds her dear conqueror against her, and begs him to be quiet.

But behind the secret door that has just has just slid aside, the old fakir Brahms appears, smiling, holding and brandishing in his hands, jaundiced by time, a dusty manuscript.

The Empress frowns. "Why, Brahms, have you come?"

With a finger over his wrinkled mouth, the fakir, respectfully, begs Djila to listen to him.

He approaches the two bewildered lovers, looks at them with infinity in his gaze, and prostrates himself on a carpet in which its weaver, during years of labor, has imprisoned roses.

"The gods, O Majesty, have granted the wish of the Empress your mother. Blessed be the gods of the Emerald Palace. The destinies foreseen by the mysterious books are accomplished, and amour is triumphant."

The fakir, feverishly rising to his feet, explains the enigma of the parchments that he has finally deciphered.

"Djila, of the heart of rose, Goddess most fortunate, by virtue of the virginity of Myram, by the impulse of your respective hearts, by virtue of the force of amour before hatred, by virtue of the pure impulse of the pearl fisher, the hero who has been able to reach his Sovereign, the mortal venom of your kiss has disappeared forever, and your tongue, that of the serpent gods, your ancestors, has become human and feminine."

The two lovers looked at one another, and they perceived and verified, in a new, interminable kiss, that the old fakir was telling the truth. Myram did not feel any pain, and Djila's tongue had become dainty and pink, that of a woman.

Under the benedictions of Brahms, they united their lips once again.

Then the aged fakir drew away, in order to go and announce the strange and welcome news to everyone, to the Emperor and the Slaves.

Was an era of happiness finally about to reign in the Emerald Palace?

III
Amour Triumphant

On the marble terrace, before the great hall of nacre, Djila is reposing on her diamante veils, and next to her Myram is sitting, pensive, but enjoying an infinite joy, savoring, as in a dream, a supreme happiness.

There have now been three paradisal nights during which the lovers have been intoxicated by their folly and all the wines of lust. The Empress, at the whim of the pearl fisher, dies of pleasure in his arms, and her eyelids, blued by amour, always attract more kisses in long strings.

Three peacocks with ocellated tails come to frolic on the terrace, parading their plumes and precious stones near Djila, who wakes up. And sliding her arms around the pearl fisher like scarves of flesh and garlands of roses, she whispers to him:

"O Myram! O my King . . . !"

IV
The Death of Shatavahama

The Emperor, charged with years, is walking down below in the park of enchantments, his back a trifle vaulted, alongside Brahms, who is speaking and making grand gestures. They encounter slaves in their path who prostrate themselves as they pass by. A gleam of felicity and gratitude is visible in the eyes of those poor folk, for their feet are no longer bruised by chains.

And suddenly, the Emperor with the venerable beard places his hand on the shoulder of the fakir, his old companion, his inseparable friend, and collapses, putting his other hand on his heart. Slaves run toward the august master; he is no more than a marionette collapsed on the ground, a turbaned and dislocated puppet.

Who, then, has informed the lovers?

They arrive, and as soon as they appear, the slaves prostrate themselves before them.

They acclaim the pearl fisher.

"The Emperor is dead! Long live Myram! Long live Myram!"

V

The Ten Sacred Cobras

However, for several days, rising from the low city, one of those sordid cries had been heard, sometimes more irritated, that battered the walls of the sacred palace. The fakir came, trembling, to warn the sovereigns. The handsome fisher understood those grim rumors, and his heart responded to the angry appeals of the multitude.

Since the tragic day that terminated so well, he had been living as if in a marvelous dream in which the former black tableau of his promises of vengeance had been erased. How could he satisfy, however, those thousands of men, women and children embittered by misery, whose cries of hatred reached all the way to the palace on its green crag?

Myram finally decided to reveal the cause of those murmurs. Then old Brahms drew mysterious signs on the nacre floor and waited. His visage, after a few seconds, lit up, and he asked Myram to don his fisher's garments and to put on over them imperial vestments. Djila, in the same way, was dressed for coronation.

Afterwards they followed the fakir and descended into the subterrains of the emerald rock. When they arrived at the center of a small room with walls clad in green stones, Brahms traced a cabalistic sign on the floor. One of the walls opened and they found themselves in the cavern of the sacred serpents.

They went down a few steps and saw before them ten enormous beasts entirely covered with admirable scintillating emeralds. Their bodies reared upright as soon as the three visitors came in, advancing quietly under the guidance of Brahms.

As they arrived near to an altar ornamented with the rarest precious stones, the fakir knelt down to pray. The two lovers held hands, and huddled close together, impressed by the strange spectacle. Then Brahms got up and, like an officiant, turning toward them, he said to them:

"You are here, young lovers, in the most secret of the rooms of the sacred rock. You see before you the ten cobras who have seen the gods of the emerald palace born, of whom Djila is the direct descendant. These divine beings, whose soul is devoted to you for eternity, will protect your love, which I shall bless before Them.

And, making Myram and Djila kneel down, he consecrated them before the altar and the gods, as Emperor and sacred Empress.

The gigantic serpents were still holding themselves erect, raising their glaucous eyes toward the new spouses. After having invoked their power, Brahms implored one of them to allow its tongue with flamboyant darts to be severed, in order to calm the avid and brutal crowd and protect and assure by means of that gesture the eternal happiness of Djila and Myram.

Immediately, to their amazement, they saw the enormous cables of the ten cobras undulate, crawl toward them, and the ten extended their tongues for the sacrifice requested by the fakir.

Brahms handed the sacred knife to the young Emperor. Myram took it boldly and cut cleanly, with a swift gesture, through one of the red darts that was offered to him. Ruby droplets spurted on to the floor.

Myram and Djila, grateful, piously deposited a kiss on the head of the sacred beast and returned to the Palace, thanking Lakshmi, under the eyes of Brahms, whose wrinkled eyes were tearful with happiness.

VI
The Emperor of the Pariahs

The howls of the low city reached their eyes with increasing violence. The Emerald Princess, purified by love, huddled against Myram, fearful of losing so quickly a happiness scarcely touched. All three of them, the sovereigns and the fakir, a trifle anxious in spite of the enormous wall separating them from the large crowd growling around the Palace, headed toward the tall golden entrance gate.

Brahms, the aged fakir, pressed a secret point, and the gate opened slowly. The plebeians covered the sacred rock with their swarm. When they saw the gate stir, and then open wide, turning on its powerful hinges, the cries of anger fell silent momentarily. What was about to happen? The crowd, suddenly stupefied by its audacity, gathered in a silence that chilled all the faces.

Quickly, however, Myram was recognized in his imperial splendor. Had he, then, saved the low city? Had he avenged all their mourning and insults?

There was a long, renewed explosion of frenetic acclamations. And no one was astonished by his quasi-divine ornaments, his turban diademed with sparkling gems, his magnificent necklaces and sumptuous bracelets. But a somber and dirty undulation of men, women and even children howled:

"The venomous tongue!"

"The venomous tongue!"

"The venomous tongue!"

The fakir took the new Emperor by the hand and asked him to show the people the scarlet and venomous tongue personally. Then, with a broad gesture, Myram raised his arm toward the sky and held out like an offering a dangling tongue, dead and now inoffensive.

Savage vociferations, howled by thousands of people, filled the air at the sight of that shred of red flesh flamboyant in the sunlight. And with a sure and firm hand, Myram threw that bloody trophy to that delirious vermin.

A black cloud took possession of that crimson fragment, with cries of bestial joy. Then, like the strokes of human bells, there was an immense apotheosis:

"Vive Myram!"

"Vive Myram!

"Vive Myram! Death, death to the Venomous Woman!"

Feverish hands were extended toward the liberator. And Myram recognized, amid the tumult of those somber waves, the same tearful women, satisfied in vengeance. Suddenly, he was gripped by a great pity toward those people, who were demanding blood for blood and death for death. He saw the young men of his own age, the young girls, the mature men, the old people, and the children magnifying his name. Having arrived at the summit, he did not want them to live in hatred of what is, of that which must be and remain up above.

Having made a sign to the humble, his former comrades, to come a little closer, he took off his adornments, removed his precious necklaces, in order to offer them the diamonds and the pearls. And there was a fantastic rush toward the gold, the wealth, the pebbles made by the sun, the topazes, the rubies, the sapphires and the emeralds. The screams for blood were changed into cries of joy.

Having no more jewels, he took off his vestments of gold and silk, and distributed them like the rest to his former brethren. As before, stripped of everything, he was no longer anything but the pearl fisher. Then he placed the palms of both his hands on his forehead, and then on his heart, and with a slow and harmonious movement, he held them up lightly toward the people.

And the sun, between his erect fingers, put the pink fire of a dawn: that of new times.

By what sudden, unanimous inspiration did the people clamor, on impulse, as if with a single formidable voice, in three salvoes:

"Vive the Emperor of the Pariahs!"

"Praise and glory to Myram!"

"Vive! Vive the liberator!"

Then Myram showed, with a sovereign gesture, in the frame of the tall golden gate, Djila, in the dazzling costume of the Princess of the Sun. The exquisite and magical Empress was weeping and smiling before so much generosity, *which was now permitted to her.*

And in his paltry costume, the pearl fisher who had gone before the Most Beautiful and the Inaccessible,

whom he had conquered, took her by the hand and proclaimed in a resounding voice:

"My friends, I present to you your queen, *transformed by
love and pity!*"

Meanwhile, Djila, divine and mischievous, tiaraed with
diamonds and golden roses, blew kisses to the people, like
Kama, the lord of caresses, directing his arrows tipped
with flowers at the world. She was seen to round out her
mouth and to dart between her red lips a delightful and
dainty tongue—one might have thought it the voluptuous
arm of Lakshmi. The Empress stuck out that tongue
adorably, according to the religious precepts, and all the
people were ecstatic before that pretty, sacred and pert
majesty. Djila thus gave those unfortunates the illusion of
her kisses, and the proof that her nature had changed.

VII
The Felicity of Believers

Then the acclamations of all that human distress, moving
in its sentiments, rose toward the lovers and toward the
Sun, whose globe, unsustainable by sight, made the sky
a quivering blue canopy. Myram and Djila, moving their
visages closer together, married their lips in the union of
all hearts. After which, solemnly, to its grandiose, ardent
celestial music, they went back into the temple, of which
the poor, before the golden gates slowly closed, were able
to glimpse the magnificence.

And to conclude this story, here, in a continuity of
images, is a crystal bathing-pool ornamented with opals.
In the transparent water, red and gold fish are moving
back and forth, with rainbow reflection, their velvety and

lacy fins fluttering like wings. The pearl fisher, amused to be still in his poor costume of old, is trying to catch the magnificent fish at the end of a precious thread attached to a cork. In the reflective water, the face of Djila, tiaraed in roses, is stirring, and the lips of the adorable young empress, happy and smiling, fasten upon her husband's mouth.

Meanwhile, the humble, agitating palms that they had collected along the road, were praying and singing hymns for the happiness of their new master. And because one of them, a young man, a handsome pearl fisher, departing from the lowest rank, ennobled by his ambition and his heroism, had now entered into the lineage of the gods; because he had risen to the throne, near to Brahma, Siva and Vishnu, among the Suns, those poor people going down all the paths of the emerald rock, going along the shore of the shining lake like a column of ants, ready to return to their hovels, their tawdry huts, their labor and their nets, imagined that their poverty was not as great henceforth, for them, and all over the world.[1]

First light was about to give way to the dawn.

Then Scheherazade stood up—unless it was the fay Lumière[2] of the marvelous lamp—and said:

"The tale is finished, and the storyteller is now silent."

---

1 Although readers are bound to wonder (are we not?) whether anyone is going to bother to tell Dao—surely the real hero of the tale—what happened to Yailee—surely the real heroine—and how he is likely to feel about his sister-in-law, given that.

2 Although the reference can be construed literally, Lumière meaning Light, it is obviously intended to invoke the Lumière brothers, inventors of the cinematograph and pioneers of the French cinema.

162

A PARTIAL LIST OF SNUGGLY BOOKS

9 781943 813513